AMISH DAISY

AMISH LOVE BLOOMS BOOK 3

SAMANTHA PRICE

AMISH ROMANCE

CHAPTER 1

"*D*aisy May Yoder!"

Daisy cringed when she heard her mother's shrill voice calling to her from the kitchen. It was never good when *Mamm* used her full name. "I'll be right there, *Mamm!*"

"That's what you said five minutes ago. I need you here *now!*"

Knowing her mother wasn't going to give up, she stomped down the stairs. It was Tuesday, and every Tuesday her mother sent her and her twin sister, Lily, around the community with food for anyone who was ill, elderly, or for some reason couldn't get food for themselves. Lily had already left the house earlier to take a chicken meal to old Mary Stoltzfus, and now the second buggy was hitched and waiting outside for Daisy to take some food to recently widowed Valerie Miller.

It wasn't that she didn't want to take the food to Valerie; it was just that—what could she possibly say to her? Dirk Miller's funeral was only a week ago. He'd

1

drowned in a nearby river, and Daisy had heard talk that Dirk had taken his own life. In Daisy's opinion he'd never looked a happy man.

"There you are," her mother said when Daisy entered the kitchen. Nancy Yoder looked her daughter up and down. "You look tidy enough, but you've got to put a smile on that face of yours."

"I can't smile when I see Valerie. Her husband's just died and she's all alone. She's probably wishing she died too. What's she got to live for now? She's so old and she wouldn't have anything to look forward to. She's got no *kinner,* so obviously, she'll never have any *grosskin.*"

"Nonsense! She's younger than me and she would've adjusted a long time ago when she knew she wasn't able to have *kinner.* Old people have a right to live, too. Life isn't just for the young, even though you young people tend to think that way."

"Well, you don't seem as old as she is."

"I am, every bit."

"What am I supposed to say to her?" Daisy whined, hoping her mother would roll her eyes at her and say she'd go instead.

"Just say that I sent you over with food. You don't have to stay long. In fact, with your attitude it's probably better that you don't. She's already upset, and we don't want her to get worse."

"Okay." Daisy blew out a deep breath. It was clear her mother was intent on staying put and not going anywhere. "I won't stay long."

"It's in that basket over there. And if you're not going

to stay and talk to her, come right back—don't dillydally along the way."

"What time will Lily be back?"

Her mother had recently started giving the twins things to do separately, and Daisy and Lily knew that she was doing it because one day they'd get married and have to live separately. Their mother had never told them that she was doing that, but they knew exactly how she thought. What their mother didn't know was that they were going to marry twins and live in one large house with all of their children, who would also be several sets of twins.

"Lily will be back when she gets here and not a minute before. Off you go. I can't stand around talking all day. I've got things to do."

"Okay, but what if Valerie cries or something?"

"She won't cry. Her husband's been dead a week already. If she does, just give her a hug."

Daisy frowned at her mother. "Oh, is that all the time you'd take to get over *Dat* dying, just a week?"

Her mother frowned back at her and her mouth turned down at the corners. "Don't say things like that."

"I wasn't saying anything mean. I don't know. I've never been in love, but I would've thought Valerie would maybe take years to get over it. I thought she'd be crying every day for ages."

"*Jah*, but she won't cry when she sees a pretty young woman at her door with food. Now go!"

Recognizing her mother's angry tone, Daisy grabbed the handle of the food basket and wasted no time in getting out of the house.

. . .

NANCY YODER GRABBED a handkerchief from up her sleeve and dabbed at her eyes. With her husband's recent heart problems, she was scared that one day she'd be alone just like her good friend Valerie Miller. It was her biggest fear. At least her husband, Hezekiah, was now well enough to go back to work on his brother's farm, but only if he did 'light' work.

The next thing she had to do was find husbands for the twins, like she'd done for Rose and Tulip, her older daughters. Nancy shook her head, almost feeling sorry for the men who'd end up with Daisy and Lily as wives. What kinds of men would find the twins appealing? They were pretty enough, but at the same time they were immature and silly and showed no signs of growing up.

When Nancy heard the horse trotting rather than walking away from the house, she ran to the front door, looked down the driveway, and yelled, "Not too fast, Daisy!"

When the horse didn't slow down, Nancy knew Daisy was pretending she couldn't hear her. *I'm going to look at that horse when she gets home and if she's driven that horse too hard, I'm going to ban her from driving the buggy for a month,* Nancy thought as she closed the front door. The girls had been told to walk the horse down the driveway and only trot the horse when they got onto the road.

Daisy and Lily were identical twins, and they had given her more than a few problems over the years. They were impulsive, headstrong, and extremely stubborn.

. . .

ON THE WAY to Valerie's house, Daisy considered throwing the contents of the basket in the tall grass along the roadside and not going at all, but her mother would find out—somehow, some way, she always did.

Going to see Valerie was a job for her mother or someone older, Daisy was certain of that.

CHAPTER 2

*D*aisy pulled up her horse outside the home of their newly widowed neighbor, Valerie Miller. Still not knowing exactly what she'd say, she jumped out of the buggy and pulled the basket along with her, settling the handle over her arm.

She rolled the small pebbles of the driveway under her feet as she trudged to the front door. Just when she thought that Valerie might not be home, she heard voices coming from inside the house. If Valerie had visitors, she wouldn't have to stay too long.

Daisy knocked on the door, and when it opened, she found she was looking at a man's chest. Slowly, she worked her way up to see a pair of unusual amber-colored eyes looking back at her.

"Is Valerie in?" Daisy finally asked.

"She is. Come inside. I'm Bruno Weber."

She stepped inside when he stepped back to allow her in. "Hello, I'm Daisy Yoder."

He held out his hand and she shook it. "Pleased to

meet you."

"And you as well." His hand was warm and large and it unnerved her slightly the way the man kept his eyes locked onto hers.

"Valerie's in here." He led the way into the living room.

Valerie stood up when she saw Daisy. "It's nice to see you."

"Hello, Mrs. Miller. My *mudder* sent me over ... I think it's chicken casserole." She held up the basket.

"That's lovely of her. Bruno, can you take that from Daisy and put it in the kitchen?"

Daisy knew that Valerie must have heard her greet Bruno at the door, otherwise, she wouldn't have been able to tell if she was Daisy or Lily. Only their close family members knew which twin was which.

Bruno nodded, took the basket from her, and left the room.

"Come and sit by me, Daisy. Tell me some happy news."

Daisy sat down beside her, feeling awkward. Her mother should've been the one to visit. "I'm sorry about what happened ... you know..."

"*Denke.* You're a sweet girl to visit an old lady."

"You're not old!" Daisy said, completely contradicting her comments in the earlier conversation she'd had with her mother.

"That's what I keep telling her," Bruno said when he came back into the room.

"Daisy, this is my youngest *bruder.*"

"Oh, hello. I didn't realize."

"I tried to get back here for the funeral, but one thing

after another kept me in Ohio."

"You're from Ohio?"

He nodded as he sat on the couch opposite. "I'm visiting Valerie for a few weeks. I'm trying to talk her into coming back with me to live permanently."

"And I'm trying to talk *him* into moving here."

Daisy nodded. It was awkward talking to people without her twin sister there beside her. They'd always been together. Lily and she had separate bedrooms, but apart from that, they were with each other all day every day until recently when their mother thought she was being smart by giving them separate errands.

"Daisy's *vadder* is the deacon."

"Is he?" Bruno asked.

Daisy nodded and wondered what she should say. Normally Lily would speak and then she'd say something, or the other way around. *Say something!* she silently screamed in her own head. "And do you like chicken, Mrs. Miller?"

"I do. Be sure to thank your *mudder* for me. Did you help her cook it?"

Daisy nodded. *"Jah,* Lily and I help our mother cook." She glanced at the good-looking man staring at her. Why couldn't she think of something interesting to talk about?

"Do you live close by, Daisy?" he asked.

"Jah, not too far away. What kind of work do you do, Bruno?" she asked, not really caring about the answer, but knowing that was one of the usual questions people ask when they meet someone for the first time.

"I'm a horse trader. I run auctions too."

"That sounds like fun."

He laughed. "It can be sometimes. Mainly it's a lot of hard work. And what do you do?"

"I haven't got a job or anything like that. I stay at home and do work there."

"Daisy's *mudder* is very busy. She's the main woman in the community, the one who does everything."

"*Jah*, she's very *gut* at arranging everything. She's always doing the organizing at all the weddings and charity events."

"And do you take after her?"

Daisy recoiled. "*Nee!* Not at all."

Bruno laughed again.

The man was so handsome and so lovely that Daisy knew that if God had been listening to her prayers, the man would have a twin for Lily. She would marry him, and Lily could marry his twin brother. She'd never felt an attraction to a man like this before. "Do you have a twin?" she asked, staring at him.

He drew his dark eyebrows together. "*Nee*. Do I look like someone you've seen before?"

Daisy could barely speak as she watched his full lips form every syllable.

"I think what Daisy means to say is that she's a twin— an identical one."

His face lit up. "There's another young woman just like you?"

"*Nee*, there's not."

Valerie said, "What do you call Lily, then?"

"Who?" Daisy asked, a little annoyed that Valerie was interrupting when she was getting along so well with Bruno.

"Lily, your twin *schweschder.*"

"Lily? Is she here?" Daisy frowned. She hadn't heard a buggy pull up.

Valerie smiled at her. *"Nee,* I think you came alone, didn't you?"

"Ach, jah."

Daisy noticed Bruno put his hand over his mouth to stifle a laugh, but she didn't care. She was lost in a world where it wouldn't matter if nothing existed except Bruno. If only they could be alone, so she could find out all about him.

"Daisy, does your *mudder* need the basket back today?"

"Huh?" Daisy thought hard. Basket? What basket was Valerie talking about? "Oh, the basket. *Nee,* she doesn't need it back. I could come and collect it tomorrow."

"Jah, do that." Bruno was now staring at her just as much as she'd been staring at him. "What time might you come back here?" he asked.

"Ten in the morning."

Valerie interrupted again. "Daisy, would you like to come back for dinner tonight?"

This time, Valerie wasn't being so annoying. "If that's not too much trouble, I'd love to."

"It's no trouble at all. What's one more for dinner? We'd enjoy the company."

"I'll bring dessert," Daisy said.

"Bring Lily too," Valerie said.

She was back to being annoying. Daisy thought quickly. "Lily won't be able to make it. She's busy tonight, but I'll be here. I could even come back early to help you, Mrs. Miller."

Bruno nodded. *"Jah,* my *schweschder* would like that."

Daisy rose to her feet. "I should go." If she was coming back there tonight, she didn't want to outstay her welcome.

"I'll walk you out," Bruno said, bounding to his feet.

"I'll see you tonight, Daisy," Valerie said.

Daisy offered her a bright smile and then stepped outside with Bruno. "How is she coping?" she asked Bruno.

"She's doing okay. It was a shock for everyone that he died so unexpectedly."

"I wouldn't like Valerie to move away. She has a lot of friends here. There are a lot of women her age."

"Jah, but they're probably married with families to look after. Valerie's got no *kinner* and no relatives."

"She'll be taken care of and my *mudder* is close to her age and there are so many people who'd miss her if she left. Everyone likes her. She's so kind and lovely."

He nodded as they continued walking to her buggy. "That's nice of you to say so."

"It's true."

When they reached the buggy, he said, "I'll see you later this evening."

"Jah, I'll be back in plenty of time to help Valerie cook. Or to cook for her."

He chuckled. "I'll look forward to it."

Daisy climbed into the buggy and then looked back and gave him a big smile. He grabbed the lower section of the reins and turned the horse until he was faced back down the driveway.

CHAPTER 3

*D*aisy arrived home and couldn't remember how she'd gotten there. She was too busy thinking about the man she had just met. He was different from the men in her community, and she was sure that he liked her, too, because he kept smiling at her. She jumped out of the buggy and unhitched the horse just the way her father had shown her.

"What took you so long?"

Daisy glanced up at her mother who was walking through the barn toward her.

"Was I a long time?"

"Considering you said you weren't staying, you were."

"That's because Valerie had a visitor and she asked me to stay. I couldn't be rude." Daisy continued talking as she gave Damon, the black horse, a rubdown. "Anyway, you didn't say you were in a hurry for me to come back."

"I was. But you're right. I didn't tell you because I didn't need you to come back, but because of what you said I expected you earlier." Nancy looked over the horse carefully. "At least you didn't drive the horse too hard this time." When Nancy had finished running her hands over the horse's legs, she straightened up. "Valerie asked you to stay? Who were her visitors?"

"There was only one; her *bruder* from Ohio."

"Hmm, from the look on your face, I'm guessing he was young and handsome?"

"He's not married." Daisy giggled. "He's a bit older than me. They asked me to come back and have dinner with them tonight."

"'They,' or Valerie's *bruder*?"

Daisy looked at her mother and knew *Mamm* could see right through her. She couldn't put anything over on her. "Valerie asked me, and I said I'd bring dessert." Daisy couldn't remember if she'd said that, but if she hadn't, she should've. Anyway, she couldn't turn up empty-handed.

"I'm glad you offered to bring dessert. She shouldn't be entertaining; that's a lot of hard work."

"That's what I thought, so I also said I'd go early to help her cook dinner."

"Good girl. Finish with Damon and I'll figure out what you can take for dessert."

"*Denke, Mamm.*"

Daisy couldn't get the smile off her face. She knew that her mother was going to make the dessert for her to take and her mother was a very good cook.

Glancing at the horse in the other stall, she knew that Lily was already home and, judging by the look of the horse, she'd been home for some time. She finished rubbing Damon down and headed into the house to tell her twin sister her news about meeting her future husband. She hoped Lily would take the news well. Bruno didn't have a twin and they'd agreed to only marry twins, or at the very least, brothers close in age. Maybe Bruno had a brother; that might soften the blow for Lily. Lily could marry Bruno's brother. She'd have to find out tonight over dinner how many single brothers he had.

She scraped the dirt off her feet before she walked into the mudroom to wash her hands. Once she dried them, she opened the back door to look for Lily.

Lily was sitting at the kitchen table eating a sandwich and their mother was nowhere about.

Lily looked up at her. "Where have you been?"

"I was visiting Valerie Miller. The one whose husband just died."

"Yeah, I know Valerie. We went to Dirk's funeral a week ago."

"That's right. Anyway, her *bruder* from Ohio is there staying with her."

"So that's where you've been for all this time? I've done three times the work while you've been sitting down talking, probably eating cake and having a *gut* time." Lily took another bite of her sandwich.

Daisy sat down next to her. "You should've seen Valerie's *bruder*."

Lily swallowed her mouthful. "Oh, is that why you took your time?"

"*Jah.* Valerie invited me back there for dinner. And I really want to go."

"What's he like? Tell me everything." Lily pushed her half-eaten sandwich away.

Daisy hoped that Lily would be happy for her. If their

15

situations were reversed, she'd be worried that she hadn't met the man her sister was interested in. "He's ... I don't know."

"You must know. You've just seen him."

"He has amber eyes and full lips. That's all I remember. I'm certain he likes me. He was pleased when Valerie asked me to come back and have dinner with them."

"Did they invite me as well? Surely they would've."

"Sorry, but I guess she didn't think of it. She's under stress with her husband just dying and everything."

"First *Mamm* gives us separate things to do and now you're getting invitations that don't include me. Now you've met a man and I haven't. Tell me he's a twin at least."

There it was. It was like they were moving apart. Daisy knew Lily wasn't happy by the way her eyes had formed into narrow slits. "He doesn't have a twin."

"What do you mean he's not a twin? How could you even like him? That's just wrong. We planned on marrying twins."

"Shh. *Mamm* will hear you. Let's go up and talk in my room before she comes back and gives us more chores."

The twins raced up the stairs and then sat cross-legged on Daisy's bed.

"But we don't even know if there are any twins our age," Daisy said. "That's the problem. Even *Dat* doesn't know of any and he nearly knows everyone in the whole country."

"He couldn't nearly know everyone in the country."

"Near enough," Daisy said.

Lily pouted, and then continued with her objections.

"I'm sure there's tons of them somewhere in all the communities across the whole country. There'd have to be. *Dat* said he'd ask around for us."

"I'd rather not marry at all than move a hundred miles away from everyone we know just for the silly idea of marrying twins." When Lily didn't respond, Daisy felt bad and looked down at her hands.

Lily groaned. "Silly now, is it? When did it become silly? The moment you met Valerie's *bruder?*"

"I'm sorry. I can't help liking him."

Slowly, Lily nodded. "You can't help who you fall in love with, I guess."

"I've only just met him. I might find out tonight that he's totally unsuitable."

Lily said, "Or you might fall in love with him. Don't mind me, I'm just being selfish. I guess … I guess I'll get used to the idea. But if you marry him, who will I marry?"

Daisy smiled and straightened up. "He could have a friend, and tonight I'm going to find out if he has a *bruder* close to his age. Don't worry." She reached forward and patted her twin on her knee.

"What time do you have to be there?"

"I said I'd be there early to help, and I've got to make dessert too, or help *Mamm* with it if she makes it."

"You better get downstairs and see what ingredients *Mamm* has for dessert. Have *her* make it and tell him you made it." Lily giggled.

Daisy's face lit up. "I'm already way ahead of you on that one. I'm glad you don't mind about Bruno."

"Are you certain he likes you too?"

"Yeah, why wouldn't he?"

Both girls giggled.

"Now to break the news to *Mamm* and *Dat*. What if they don't allow you to go?" Lily asked.

"Why wouldn't they? *Mamm's* already said it's okay."

"Really? I suppose that's because we've behaved lately and haven't gotten into trouble over anything in months."

They certainly had done everything that had been asked of them. Even helping their mother with her duties of helping people. That had to make her mother feel kindly toward her.

"Where is *Mamm* anyway?" Lily asked.

"I don't know. I saw her when I came home," Daisy said.

"Let's go find her."

When they walked back into the kitchen, their mother was right there waiting for them. "Where have you been, Lily? I heard you come home and then you disappeared. I was calling out to you."

"Oh, I didn't hear. We were up in Daisy's room just then," Lily answered.

"Cleaning your rooms, did you say?" Nancy asked.

From the tone of her mother's voice, Daisy knew she wasn't in a good mood.

"Actually, I was looking for you when I came home, *Mamm*. Where were you?" Lily asked. "I came home before Daisy and couldn't see you anywhere."

"You didn't look too far. I was in the vegetable garden seeing if anything had survived the frost we got the other night. Now, how did you two go on your outing?" she asked Lily.

"Fine," Lily said. "Daisy went to Valerie's and she has her *bruder* there from Ohio, and—"

"She only had one *schweschder* here for the funeral." Her mother looked at Daisy.

Daisy could see her mother was already forming an opinion of Bruno. *"Jah,* he said he couldn't get there. Anyway, he's there now keeping Valerie company. Don't forget about the dessert, *Mamm.*"

"I won't forget. Are you sure Bruno didn't invite you? I hope Valerie's well enough for visitors."

Her mother peered at her with her mouth drawn tight. That meant that there was only one right answer and she hoped she'd make the right one. "Honestly, it was Valerie herself who invited me. I was worried about all the work, so that's when I said I'd come back early to help."

"Good."

Daisy licked her lips. Going to Valerie's early meant that she'd have less time to do chores about the house. "I mean, she's just lost her husband and things must be hard for her."

"Well, why wouldn't she eat the chicken casserole you took her?" *Mamm* asked.

"Oh, I don't know. I didn't think of that."

Her mother breathed out heavily and looked up at the ceiling. "That would make sense to me. Unless she intends to freeze it and eat it another time." She glanced at Lily, and then set her eyes back onto Daisy. "Did she only invite you?"

"Jah."

"I'm pleased that you said you'd help her. That was kindhearted."

Daisy smiled, pleased to be getting praise from her mother for something. While the going was good, she added, "I also said I'd bring dessert."

"You don't have to keep reminding me. I've been thinking about that and you can take the cherry pie I made yesterday. I was going to have one of you take it to old Mary tomorrow, but I'll find something else for Mary."

Lily grunted. "We don't have to go visiting again tomorrow, do we? I thought we only did that one day a week."

"We do it whenever we can. It's time effective to do it one day a week, but sometimes it's not always going to work like that. I just found out that Mary's not well."

"That's bad news about Mary. You really don't mind if I go tonight?"

"I already said you could. It's strange that she didn't invite your *schweschder*."

Lily piped up. "That's what I thought."

"We're two separate people. You're giving us things to do separately. Lily wasn't there, so Valerie just didn't think about her."

"I think it had more to do with Bruno," Lily said with a pout.

Daisy glared at her sister. She had casually mentioned to her mother that Valerie had her brother staying with her, but she didn't want her mother's overactive mind too focused on Bruno.

"Bruno?" Her mother glared at Daisy.

"*Jah*, Valerie's *bruder*."

"From Ohio," Lily added.

Daisy frowned at Lily, causing Lily to pull a face back at her, all without their mother noticing.

"What's he like, this *bruder* of Valerie's?" Their mother sat down at the kitchen table and the girls sat down too.

"Full lips and amber eyes is what she told me." Lily cackled an evil laugh.

"She asked me, not you," Daisy said, annoyed with her sister for a third time in less than two minutes. She could only figure that Lily was jealous, but why ruin things for her? Lily had made her sound foolish as well.

"Interesting. And the age of this young full-lipped, amber-eyed man?"

"I didn't ask." Daisy was only thankful she didn't tell Lily too much else.

Their mother leaned forward as though she was only just getting started. "Single?"

"*Jah,* he had no *fraa* with him and he's got no *baard.*"

Lily giggled again.

Their mother ignored Lily, still focused on Daisy and finding out more about the young man and his marriage worthiness. "What job does he have?"

"He said something about horse auctions. I wasn't really listening."

"He's an auctioneer?"

From her mother's tone, she seemed impressed that he was an auctioneer. Daisy shook her head. "I don't know if that's what he said exactly, but he said something about horse auctions."

"He probably goes around with a scoop and cleans up all the horse manure at the auctions," Lily suggested. "That's working at horse auctions."

"That's not nice, Lily," Daisy said.

"Well, for all you know that's what he could do. There are dozens of jobs at horse auctions. Clean out your ears next time, Daisy," Lily said. "Do that before you go there tonight so you can answer all *Mamm's* questions."

"Lily, I'm trying to find out a few things and you're not helping."

"Sorry, *Mamm.*"

"Just be quiet while I'm talking to Daisy for just one minute."

"I'll try. It won't be easy, but I'll try."

Nancy turned her attention back to Daisy. "Valerie wouldn't have invited you back if she didn't appreciate you going there. You must've been a comfort to her."

"She's a lovely person. I like Valerie, and I always have."

"I'll have your *vadder* drive you there."

"*Nee,* don't do that. I said I'd go there early to help."

"Your *vadder* will be home early today."

"Why?" Lily asked.

"He's finishing earlier now the weather's getting so cold."

Daisy would feel awful if she arrived there driven by her father as though she were a child. "*Nee, Mamm,* I can drive myself. It's not even that far."

"Well, we'll see what he says when he gets home. If he's too tired, he might let you go alone."

There was no use saying anything further. If she protested too much, her mother would only dig her heels in further. She wanted Bruno to see her as an adult. Only a child would have their father drive them places.

. . .

22

As Daisy had feared, her father insisted on driving her to Valerie's house. It was obvious that her mother had whispered to him that Valerie's brother was staying there, and that Daisy liked him.

"I'll come in for a minute and say hello," her father said when they pulled up outside Valerie's house.

"Of course you will," Daisy said under her breath. It was embarrassing that her father was dropping her off and then collecting her later. To make things worse, he was coming inside deliberately to meet Bruno.

Furious at her mother's meddling, she buried her feelings and fixed a smile on her face so Bruno wouldn't think she was a grumpy person. She couldn't let Bruno see that small things angered her so much. He could find that out after they were married.

Hezekiah Yoder knocked on the door of Valerie's house and Bruno opened the door.

"*Dat*, this is Bruno, Valerie's *bruder*."

They shook hands.

"I'm Hezekiah Yoder."

"*Jah*, Daisy's *vadder*. I'm pleased to meet you. Will you be joining us for dinner too?"

"*Nee, denke*. I'm just bringing Daisy and I thought I'd come in and see how Valerie's doing."

"Come right in," Bruno said, opening the door wide and stepping back to let them through.

Her father walked in first, and Bruno gave Daisy a big smile.

"I'll take the dessert to the kitchen," Daisy said, walking past him.

"Hezekiah, it's nice to see you," Daisy heard Valerie say

from the kitchen. She stayed there to see what else she would hear.

Just as she stepped closer to listen in, Bruno walked into the kitchen and she nearly bumped into him.

"I can take you home after dinner, Daisy. There's no need for your *vadder* to come back and collect you late at night. Valerie told me he hasn't been well."

"That's nice of you. Perhaps you can suggest that to him before he leaves? If I mention it, he'll reject the idea."

"I'll insist I take you home." He looked over at the basket and smiled. "And what did you make for dessert?"

She took Lily's advice and carefully chose her words so he'd think she'd made it. "We have cherry pie for dessert."

"That's one of my favorites and barely anyone makes them nowadays. What a delight." He smiled at her and her heart melted. "I suppose we should join them," he said.

"Do we have to?"

He laughed. *"Jah.* Come on."

They sat down with Hezekiah and Valerie. Ten minutes later, Hezekiah stood up and announced he'd collect Daisy at nine thirty.

Bruno bounded to his feet. "You shouldn't have to come out so late. I'll take Daisy back to your *haus.* It's no trouble. I need to give Valerie's horse some exercise since Valerie hasn't been out for some days."

"Is that so, Valerie?"

"Jah, I was just asking Bruno today if he'd take the horse out soon."

"As long as it's no trouble for you, Bruno," Hezekiah said.

"You'd be doing me a favor, Hezekiah, really you would," Valerie said.

Daisy held her breath. She could tell her father was weighing things up in his mind, like what Daisy's mother would say when she found out he wasn't going back to collect her.

Hezekiah nodded. "I'll see you when you get home, Daisy." He looked at Bruno and Valerie. "Enjoy the cherry pie. It's a recipe that's been handed down and my wife bakes the cherry pies so well."

Daisy bounded to her feet and slipped her arm around her father's, walking him to the door. *"Jah,* and there's nothing I like more than trying out all those old *familye* recipes—like that cherry pie. *Gut nacht, Dat."*

Her father turned around at the door and stared at his daughter.

"Gut nacht, Hezekiah," Valerie called out.

"I won't bring her home late, Mr. Yoder."

Hezekiah nodded and with gentle pressure on his arm from Daisy, he was further out the door. Daisy closed the door behind him and walked back to Valerie. "Now, how can I help you with the dinner?"

"If it's all right with you, we're going to have that chicken casserole your *mudder* was kind enough to send over with you earlier today."

"I don't mind at all. That's a good idea."

Bruno said, "I was at the markets early today and picked up plenty of fresh bread too."

"Good. Can I help you with anything else, Valerie?"

"Nee. All I have to do is heat up the food. I'm sorry to get you over here so early."

Daisy smiled, thinking of all the chores at home she missed out on. Besides that, it gave her more time with Bruno. "I don't mind at all. Do you have chores or house-work I can do for you before dinner?"

"That's a kind offer. There's nothing to do. I've been able to do things. Keeping busy has helped me keep my mind off other things."

Bruno said, "Valerie likes to keep busy. She hasn't been out because she's had visitors coming and going with people stopping by to pay their respects."

Daisy wondered when dinner would be ready. It was awkward just sitting there trying to think of conversation. She could've talked to Bruno if they'd been alone and she wasn't sure what to say to Valerie. Finally she said, "You must have something I can help with."

"I can't think of anything. Why don't you relax and talk with Bruno and I'll make us a cup of tea." Valerie stood up and Daisy sprang to her feet.

"I can do it."

"Nee. You sit and I'll get you tea. It's still too early for dinner and tea won't ruin our appetites."

Valerie left the room and now Daisy smiled at Bruno who was staring at her.

"Did you make the cherry pie?" he asked.

Daisy was taken aback. Could he read her mind? It was a strange thing to ask and she didn't want to lie to him just in case he might be her future husband. *"Nee,* my *mudder* made it. She's an excellent baker. I hope I'm as good as she is one day."

He laughed.

"What's funny?"

"Nothing at all. I'm just happy. Happy to have met someone my age. I'm glad Valerie invited you to dinner. I'm looking forward to finding out more about you."

"There's not much to know."

"I think there's a lot more to you. You're intriguing."

A giggle escaped her lips. She loved the attention he was giving her. "What would you like to know?"

"You said you live close by?"

"*Jah*, you'll see tonight when you drive me home that it's not that far."

"What sort of things are you interested in?"

"Just the normal things. I like baking and sewing."

"Do you sew quilts?"

"We used to a few years back. When I was younger, we all worked on one together. That's my two older sisters, my twin, and *Mamm*."

"Do you have brothers?"

"Two. The oldest in the family are boys. They're both married."

"And the rest are married?"

"*Nee*, I'm not married and neither is my twin *schweschder*."

"Ah, the lucky last in the family."

"And the youngest." Daisy giggled. "If I said something about being lucky in front of my *vadder*, I'd get a lecture that there's no such thing as luck."

Bruno nodded. "I was trying to be funny. Thanks for telling me. I'll watch what I say around him."

That was the right answer as far as Daisy was concerned. He showed he had it in his mind that he'd be around her father, and that meant he was interested in her, she was certain of that. "And what do you like doing, Bruno?"

"I like my work and that keeps me busy."

"That's a good thing." If only she could remember what he said that he did for a living. Was it horse trading, or something to do with horse auctions? She was sure he said something about horse auctions because that's what she told Lily, or was it her mother she told? Since she'd met him just a few hours ago, she couldn't concentrate on anything. Did that mean she was in love?

Valerie came back into the room. "Here we go." She placed a tray of tea items on the table near the couch.

"I could've helped you with that, Valerie," Bruno said.

"Or I could've," Daisy said.

"It's fine. It wasn't that heavy." She sat back down on the couch. "Milk or sugar, Daisy?"

"Just black for me, *denke.*"

"And you, Bruno?"

"However it comes, as long as it's not too sweet."

Valerie poured the tea from a teapot and handed them a cup of tea each before she settled back down on the couch with a cup for herself. After she had taken a sip, she said, "My late husband gave me that teapot." She looked downward. "Oh, it sounds funny to call him my late husband."

Daisy felt awkward and looked at the large white teapot. "What a nice teapot. It's a lovely shape."

"*Denke.*"

Daisy couldn't believe she'd picked the teapot to talk about. Amish wedding gifts were always practical things. Daisy recalled that her father gave her mother a treadle sewing machine for a wedding gift and it still worked as perfectly as the day he bought it. Daisy and all her sisters had learned to sew on it. She didn't mention it to Valerie because she didn't want to make her sad. A sewing machine seemed a lot better gift than a teapot.

Valerie continued, *"Jah.* He surprised me with it. We'd been shopping weeks before we married, looking for something. I forget what it was we were shopping for. I admired the teapot, but it was too expensive and I never thought another thing about it. It just showed how thoughtful and caring he was." Valerie took another sip and looked at Daisy. "I hope you don't mind me talking about him. It helps to talk."

"I don't mind at all. I didn't think you'd want to talk about him." Daisy hadn't been around death. Both sets of grandparents had died before she was born and apart from people she knew in the community who'd died, she'd never lost anyone close to her.

"It helps. It makes me feel like he's still around. I feel like he is. I expect to see him walking through the door at any moment. It doesn't seem real that he's gone."

Daisy put both hands around her teacup, wondering what words of comfort she should be uttering. Nothing came to her. She took a sip of tea, hoping someone would say something.

"I'm glad you came to dinner, Daisy. I need some fresh young company for a change."

"What does that make me then?" Bruno asked, pulling a face at his sister.

Daisy giggled.

"You don't count. You're *familye*. Daisy's always been

bright and happy." She turned away from Bruno and looked at Daisy. "Every time I see you and Lily, you're both so happy. I've never seen either of you downcast or sad."

"What's your secret, Daisy?" Bruno asked as he leaned forward.

"Secret for what?"

"The secret of happiness. It's a thing which makes many people struggle."

Daisy shrugged her shoulders. "It's just the way I am. Also, Lily makes me laugh all the time. We have a lot of fun together. I guess I make her laugh too." The mention of Lily made her feel bad that she hadn't brought her tonight too. As well as that, she felt guilty for saying that Lily was busy tonight. She hoped God wouldn't punish her for her lies.

"They say a merry heart is like a medicine," Valerie said. "You'll live to a very long age."

"I hope so." Daisy took a sip of tea, wondering what her life would be like at ninety.

"I'm going to throw myself into volunteer work to keep me busy. That'll keep my mind off my own troubles."

"What sort of things will you do?" Daisy asked Valerie.

"Just generally helping people. Things like your mother does."

"She always needs help with things."

"I'll visit her and see what I can help out with. Your *vadder* seems to have fully recovered from the scare he had a while back. Landed in hospital, didn't he?"

"*Jah*, he has a problem with his heart, but he's okay now as long as he takes the tablets every day." She turned to Bruno and explained, "We thought he was dead. He'd passed out in the living room after he had a fright."

"It must've been some fright," Bruno said. "What was it?"

Quick, change the subject. Daisy didn't want to go down that track of dredging up the dark family secrets of inappropriate men that she and her sisters might have been involved with, albeit briefly. "It might have happened anyway right at that moment. I don't think it was the fright. It must've been a fright for you, Valerie, because your husband wasn't even ill."

Valerie nodded. "That's right. I wasn't prepared. If he'd been sick or in the hospital, at least I would've known he wasn't well. To die in an accident like that was awful. I don't even know how it happened."

"The rescue people were vague in their explanations. That is, the paramedics who responded," Bruno said. "That's what Valerie told me."

"I'm very sorry, Valerie. I don't know what else to say," Daisy said.

Valerie wiped a tear from her eye. *"Denke."*

Bruno reached out a hand and touched Valerie on her shoulder. "There's nothing anyone can say, but it's touching to me and my *schweschder* that you care." Then he said to Valerie, "You wouldn't be alone if you'd come back with me."

She shook her head. "I've made a life for myself here. I don't want to start over at my age."

He slowly nodded. "The offer's always there."

"I know." She patted his hand, which was still on her shoulder.

Daisy saw what a caring man Bruno was.

A little later in the evening, Daisy helped Valerie prepare the meal while Bruno set the table. Since the meal only had to be heated, there wasn't much to do apart from set the table, slice the bread, and put some butter in a serving dish.

CHAPTER 4

"You what?" Nancy shrieked at her husband when he got home and told her he'd given permission for Bruno to bring Daisy back home.

"He said he'd bring her home," he repeated, stroking his gray beard.

Nancy took a moment to take a couple of deep, calming breaths. Her husband had heart problems, so screaming at him might not be a good idea, but couldn't he think for himself? Why did everything have to fall on her shoulders? That's how it felt. He wasn't strict enough with the girls and never had been. Girls like Lily and Daisy needed strict discipline.

She tried the calm and reasonable approach, hoping her husband would see the error of his ways. "Hezekiah, do you remember what happened the last time that Daisy was in a buggy with a man? And we kind of knew him, and this man we don't know at all."

Hezekiah frowned. "That was two years ago, Nancy.

We can't be with the girl every moment. You want Daisy to get married someday, don't you?"

"You know I do, and the sooner, the better."

"We have to let her go sometime. We can't control her —not at her age. There comes a point that we have to let go and trust. Think of it like someone putting a sailboat in the water. There can either be a storm to endure, or a gentle breeze can well up and gently guide the boat to where it's supposed to be. There isn't any way we can control the weather."

Nancy shook her head. He was never going to see things her way. Life wasn't always to be compared with sailboats and water. "Think of it this way, Hezekiah, would you put a sailboat in the water when there were black storm clouds in the sky?"

He rubbed the side of his face. *"Nee.* I wouldn't. I'd wait until the storm clouds left."

"Exactly!"

"I don't see the meaning of your story, Nancy."

"I never see the meaning of your stories!" Nancy breathed slowly to calm herself. "The twins aren't like Rose and Tulip. They're stubborn, easily led, ignorant, and impulsive. And I left out completely selfish and not to be trusted."

Hezekiah's jaw dropped open. "I think you're being harsh. They're both bright young women and they like to have excitement."

"That's your interpretation because you don't see them day in and day out. I'm the one at home with them all the time, and I know them better than you do."

"You're seeing the worst in them. They've got such good qualities—"

"I'm being realistic. I want them to be married, but they must be closely monitored. We can't leave them alone because they don't think clearly. They're easily led astray. That's why I asked you to take her there and collect her; otherwise, I never would have let her go without Lily. Now go change out of those clothes and then wash up for dinner."

"I'm sorry, dear."

"You must listen to me next time, Hezekiah."

He nodded. "I wouldn't dare not!" he murmured as he turned to get changed out of his clothes.

"What did you say?"

He turned around and smiled at her. "I will, dear."

As soon as they had said their silent prayer of thanks for the meal in front of them, Daisy was anxious to find out if Bruno had a brother. She was sure that he had a lot of siblings because she remembered that Valerie was the oldest and he was the youngest. She hoped the conversation would work its way around to the topic so she wouldn't have to ask.

"How long are you staying, Bruno?" Daisy asked casually as she buttered her bread.

"As long as my *schweschder* needs me."

Daisy looked over at Valerie and smiled.

"I shall need you for a very long time," Valerie said jokingly.

"Not if you move back to Ohio with me."

"What's so good about Ohio?" Daisy asked.

"You should come and see for yourself sometime."

"Maybe I will."

"I grew up there and so did Valerie. Valerie only moved here when she married Dirk."

Daisy's eyes flickered to Valerie to see if she minded her brother talking about her late husband after she had shed a few tears earlier. She didn't seem to.

"It's been my home ever since. I don't see any good reason to go back. It would've changed so much anyway. I'm used to being here now. All my memories are here. You should move here, Bruno," Valerie said.

"*Jah,* it's a *gut* place to live," Daisy added.

Bruno laughed. "I'm outnumbered here. It's not fair."

"Perhaps Daisy can show you around and you'll get a good idea of the place and what it's got to offer."

"I'd be only too happy to do that," Daisy said, trying to sound normal while inside she wanted to leap for joy.

He looked up from his food. "You wouldn't mind showing me around, Daisy?"

She loved the way he said her name so delicately, like butterfly wings tickling her ears. Her name had never sounded so beautiful. "I wouldn't mind one little bit."

"When might you be able to do that, Daisy? Tomorrow?" Valerie asked.

Bruno frowned at his sister. "You trying to get rid of me, sis?"

"I just want you to have a good look around, and I'm not up to showing you the sights."

"I could come back tomorrow," Daisy offered.

"I'll find out where you live tonight, and then I'll collect you tomorrow and we can explore. That'll give Valerie's horse plenty of work, too."

Daisy nodded. "Okay."

"That's settled, then," Valerie said.

Daisy smiled at Bruno and he smiled back at her. She longed to ask if he had a brother for her sister. Perhaps she could ask him tomorrow if the subject didn't come up tonight. Throughout the dinner, she used her very best table manners to make the very best impression that she could.

CHAPTER 5

*L*ater that night, Daisy was pleased to be in the buggy so close to Bruno.

"*Denke* for driving me home, Bruno."

"I'm happy to do it. It saves your *vadder* from coming back out. And, as I said, Valerie wants her horse to be worked."

"That's good."

"Are you certain it'll be okay with your parents if I take up most of your time tomorrow?"

Daisy was certain that he thought her to be much younger than she was, thanks to her father bringing her to Valerie's house. "I'm twenty-one—nearly," Daisy blurted out.

"Hmm, let me do the math. That means you're twenty, or possibly nineteen?"

"*Jah.* Something like that."

He laughed.

"And I don't need their permission," she added.

"My sisters had to ask my parents permission for

everything when they were living under our parents' roof."

"What about your brothers?" Daisy asked, hoping he'd mention someone whom Lily could marry.

"I don't have any."

"What? Not at all?"

"*Nee.* I've got ten siblings, all females. My parents were certainly hoping I was a boy. I guess I was a pleasant surprise." He chuckled again.

She stared ahead at the darkened road. Now she had to go home, and not only tell Lily that she'd fallen in love, but tell her twin sister that Bruno didn't even have a brother. "Did you have a close male friend that you grew up with and have remained friends with ever since?"

He glanced over at her. "*Jah,* how did you know?"

"Just a guess."

"His name is Joel and he just got married last month."

Daisy was devastated. Things weren't looking good for Lily. How could she go home and tell Lily about her happiness when Lily had none? They'd always shared everything, and had always done everything at the same time. It wasn't right. Perhaps Bruno wasn't the man for her after all. Both of them had prayed to marry twin brothers ever since their oldest sister, Rose, had gotten married years before.

"Things are different now between Joel and me. We used to do everything together, but now that he's married he's busy with other things."

That would happen with Lily and her if she got married and Lily didn't. "That's too bad. I didn't expect Valerie to have a *bruder* as young as you."

"She's the oldest and I'm the youngest, and there are many sisters in between, don't forget. I only have a few memories of her in the house before she got married and moved away."

"That's a bit sad."

"We've seen a fair bit of each other. She always came home for one thing or another. She has to sell the farm, and that's why I'm trying to get her to come back to Ohio with me."

"Why does she have to sell the farm?"

"When Dirk died he left debts. The *familye* designated me as the one to come out here and bring her back—try to make her see sense."

It all fitted in with the rumors Daisy had heard of Dirk doing away with himself. If there was truth in it, maybe he did it because he had huge debts and was about to lose the farm, but she never thought an Amish man would do such a thing. She kept her thoughts to herself. "Sorry to hear that. I had no idea she was about to lose the farm. Does she know? Oh, I suppose that's a silly question. Of course she'd know."

"She does."

"She doesn't seem upset about it."

"I'd say it's too much for her to face at this time."

"Maybe the community can help. We could have a fundraiser."

He glanced over at her in the semi-darkness. "Possibly."

"Shall I talk to my *vadder* about it? He could work something out with the bishop. Maybe someone could lease her land, or something."

He nodded. "That might help. *Denke*, Daisy. There are various things that she could do, but she's not in the state of mind to make decisions right now. She could sell off the land and keep the *haus*; that's the only thing I've thought of that could get her out of immediate trouble."

"That sounds like a *gut* idea."

"I need to wait until I can ask her some things. Perhaps don't talk to your *vadder* just yet."

"Okay, I won't. Oh, it's this driveway just off to the left."

When he stopped outside the house, he said, "I'm looking forward to tomorrow, Daisy. Shall I collect you at ten in the morning?"

She nodded. "Ten would be perfect." She got out of the buggy and walked toward the house. By the time she'd reached the front door, he'd turned the buggy around. She gave a wave into the darkness, not knowing if he was looking, and walked inside.

Daisy was surprised to see her mother sitting up in the chair. She'd obviously been waiting for her. "Am I late, *Mamm?*"

"*Nee.* I'm just glad you got home in one piece."

She could tell her mother was angry and she didn't know why. "Bruno drove me. He's Valerie's *bruder*. Didn't *Dat* tell you Bruno was driving me home?"

"*Jah,* I've heard all about Bruno from your *vadder*. He thinks he's a nice young man."

"He is."

"That's what everyone thought about Nathanial and look what happened there."

"That was a long time ago. And anyway, you can't keep thinking about that."

"Why wouldn't I? He caused your *vadder* to have a heart attack."

"Dat didn't have a heart attack. He had some kind of a turn."

"It was a heart attack and now he's on medication for heart disease. He doesn't need any more stress from you."

Daisy sat down next to her mother. "Do you think I caused *Dat* to have a heart attack? Is that why you've been so angry with me these past two years? Do you hate me?"

"Of course I don't hate you. *Nee,* not you; it was Nathanial."

"You hate Nathanial?"

"I don't hate anyone. You shouldn't even use that word. I suppose, to be fair, your *vadder* had underlying issues with his heart. It might have been just as well all that fuss happened so he could get on the medication."

Nathanial had taken her for a buggy ride nearly two years ago and had displayed bad behavior, causing Daisy to jump out of the buggy to escape from his advances. When she'd found her way home, her parents went wild upon seeing her walking home by herself when Nathanial should've brought her home. Her mother hadn't trusted Nathanial from the beginning because he was Jacob's brother and Jacob had treated her sister, Rose, in a cruel manner and ended up leaving her to marry someone else. Daisy had thought it wasn't fair to judge Nathanial by his brother, but as it turned out, her mother had been right all along.

"You don't need to worry about anything with Bruno. He's very trustworthy."

"Hmm, that's what your *vadder* said."

"See? It must be true." Daisy quickly added, "Valerie asked me for a favor."

"Hmm?" Her mother stared at her, waiting to find out what it was.

"She asked me if I could show her *bruder* around because she doesn't feel up to it and her horse needs exercising."

"When does she want you to do that?"

"Tomorrow at ten in the morning."

"Okay. And he's coming to fetch you?"

"*Jah.* He is."

"*Gut!* Then I can meet him too."

Daisy's jaw dropped open. She hadn't figured on that. First her father had embarrassed her and tomorrow was going to be her mother's turn. "I'm only showing him around. I don't want him to think that he's being ogled and that you are seeing if he's worthy marriage material for me."

"There's no reason he'll think any of those things. He's a visitor to the community, so why wouldn't I want to meet him?"

Daisy bit her lip. "Okay. I guess that's true."

"Don't worry so. You seem uptight about something."

From the deep lines that formed in her mother's forehead, she looked like the one uptight about something.

"*Nee,* I'm not at all. I just want to be treated as an adult. You treat me like a child and so does *Dat.* Lily and I are grown up now. Girls our age have families and husbands."

"You like him a lot, don't you?" her mother asked.

"Who?"

"Bruno."

Daisy stared at her mother, wondering if it would be okay if she told her the truth. Sometimes she felt it was better if she kept things from her mother to save a lecture. "I do like him. How can you tell?"

She saw a slight smile forming around her mother's lips. "You told me you did."

"Oh, I don't remember."

"Vagueness is a symptom of the love disease."

Daisy grimaced. "Ooh. That's not very nice to call it a disease. I don't want to have a disease."

"It's the best kind of disease someone can have."

Now her mother was being weird.

"I better get some sleep. Oh, before I forget, Valerie said she was going to come and see you to talk about her helping out with fundraisers and doing volunteer work."

"*Wunderbaar.*"

"She's trying to take her mind off Dirk."

"Keeping busy is good."

Daisy stood up and kissed her mother on the cheek before she went upstairs to tell Lily all about her night.

Lily's door was closed and she hoped her sister was still awake. She opened the door and, as she did, light flooded in from the gaslight in the hallway. "Lily, are you awake?"

Lily sat up. "I'm awake. I was trying to stay awake to hear what happened and then I fell asleep."

Daisy sat down on the edge of her sister's bed. "I'm pretty sure I'm in love, and he likes me too. He asked me to show him around. No, wait, Valerie asked me to show him around, but he seemed pretty happy about it."

Lily rubbed her eyes. "When are you doing that?"

"Tomorrow morning."

"Does *Mamm* know?"

"*Jah,* she's okay with that."

"*Gut.* You're paving the way for me. If she lets you do things, she might let me do things."

"Yeah. I already told her she treats us like we're younger than we are."

Lily whispered, "She was angry with *Dat* when he told her that Bruno was driving you home. I heard them talking."

"What did she say?"

"I can't remember exactly, but I could tell she was angry. She was using that controlled tone, like she was stopping herself from shouting."

"The one where she gets really loud and then takes a few deep breaths and starts speaking quieter than she normally does?"

Lily giggled. "That's right, that's the one."

Daisy yawned. "I had a nice night. Valerie is so lovely, and that's probably why Bruno is so nice."

"Where are you going with him tomorrow?"

"I don't know. I don't even care." Daisy pulled off her prayer *kapp* and began to unbraid her hair.

"He might care."

"We'll just drive around. He just wants to see what's around and give Valerie's horse some exercise. It's no big deal." Everyone was annoying her. "I might go to bed. It's late and I've got an early start tomorrow morning."

"Gut nacht, Daisy."

"Gut nacht." Daisy was pleased to get to the privacy of her own bedroom. This was the first thing that she could remember that she and Lily weren't sharing. She had a man she could fall in love with. It didn't seem right that her sister didn't have one too so they could share their joy and talk about things together. Lily had never been in love before, so how could Daisy feel comfortable talking to her about Bruno? It didn't feel right being happy without Lily feeling the same.

When she got back to her room, she threw her prayer *kapp* down on the dresser and picked up her hairbrush. After she brushed her long hair with a few extended strokes, she changed out of her dress and into her night-gown. Once she slipped in between the cool sheets, she put the guilt over her sister to one side and imagined what it would be like being married to Bruno. Of course, he would have to move from Ohio. She drifted off to sleep, smiling as visions of being married to Bruno, with many children, played out in her head.

CHAPTER 6

*D*aisy had woken at the crack of dawn after having dreams about Bruno. She was excited to be seeing him, for real, that morning. If she made a good effort to show how nice it was where she lived, there was a chance he might decide to stay on. Valerie had been trying to talk him into moving and she would help her. Valerie would benefit too if she had a family member close by.

"*Gut mayriye,* Daisy."

Daisy swung around and saw her father. "Morning."

He was closely followed by her mother, who always made breakfast for their father of a morning before he left for work.

"You're awake early, Daisy."

"That's because I had a good sleep."

As her father sat down at the table, he said, "Your *mudder* tells me you're showing Bruno around this morning?"

"I am. He wants to take Valerie's horse for a run, and

Valerie thought he should see what there is to see. She's trying to talk him into moving here."

"We can always do with more young men here," her mother commented as she cracked two eggs into a bowl. "Can I get you anything, Daisy?"

Daisy normally made her own breakfast. *"Nee denke.* I'll get something later."

"You can't leave home with no food in your stomach," her mother said.

"I mean later, but before he comes. Don't worry. I won't go hungry." If she stayed in the kitchen, she would be inundated with questions about Bruno. "I'll fetch the eggs." She grabbed the basket and headed outside to be faced with a cold blast of wind. Even though it was cold, she knew it would be warm in the chicken house since it was protected on one side by the barn and the other by a wall of trees. It was nearly that time of year when they needed to move the chickens into the barn.

After she took her time collecting the eggs and talking to the chickens, she headed back into the house. Her father had finished breakfast and was just about to go to work and Lily was now awake and sitting at the kitchen table.

"I collected the eggs for you, Lily. I didn't top up the food or water though."

"Denke, I'll do that later."

Daisy was a bundle of nerves and knew she'd be that way until Bruno got there. The next couple of hours were a blur of talking to Lily, eating breakfast, washing up, and then cleaning the kitchen, after which, she paced up and down past the kitchen window while waiting for Bruno to arrive. From there, she had the best view of the driveway to see him as he approached. If she was fast enough, she could leave before her mother remembered she was going to talk with him.

"He's coming!" Daisy called out in excitement, totally forgetting her earlier plans of being discreet.

Lily jumped up from the kitchen table where she'd been mending one of her dresses and stared at the approaching buggy. Her mother entered the kitchen, smiled at Daisy, and then headed for the door. At this rate, her mother would be talking with Bruno before she did. Daisy smoothed down her dress, straightened her *kapp*, and hurried to catch her mother.

Her mother walked out the front door just as Daisy reached it. Bruno jumped down from the buggy and walked toward them.

"*Guder mariye.* You must be Bruno?" her mother said in a sweet voice, walking toward him.

"*Jah,* I am, and *guder mariye* to you. You're Mrs. Yoder?"

"I am."

They smiled at each other and each gave a polite nod.

"Oh, I've got your basket in the back." Bruno reached into the buggy and pulled out the basket, handing it to Nancy.

"*Denke,*" Nancy said.

"Valerie said she'll drop the pie dish back soon, in a day or two."

"There's no rush. I have plenty," Nancy said.

Bruno's eyes traveled to Daisy, who was now standing beside her mother. "Are you ready, Daisy?"

"*Jah.* Bye, *Mamm.*" Daisy walked toward the buggy,

knowing her sister would be watching from the kitchen window. She'd find out later what Lily thought of him, but she hoped that Lily thought he was as fine as she thought him to be.

Bruno got into the seat beside her after saying a polite goodbye to her mother. "It's nice to see you again, Daisy."

"And you."

He turned the buggy to head back down the driveway. "Where to?"

"Go left. I'll show you the town center."

"I drove through it to get to Valerie's place when I arrived."

"Driving through is different from walking through. We'll start there and then I'll take you somewhere else. That's if you don't mind going for a walk."

"I don't mind at all."

As the buggy horse clip-clopped up the road, Daisy was pleased that she felt more relaxed than she had the night before.

"What was it like growing up with all girls?" Daisy asked.

He laughed. "I had a lot of *mudders*. And I had a lot of people telling me what to do."

"That doesn't sound good."

"I might have turned out a little too spoiled for my own good. Anyway, that's what my *mudder* keeps telling me. She says that's why …" He stopped abruptly.

Daisy guessed he was about to say 'that's why I'm not married.'

He continued, "That's why I'm the way I am."

"And what way is that?"

"I'm not going to tell you. You'll have to find out for yourself."

"How long will that take? I'm not a patient person."

He glanced at her. "We have something in common, then. I have no patience either. When I set my mind to something, it has to happen right away. Except, I can't be like that with Valerie. I have to wait until she sees sense and realizes she should come back home with me. I don't want her to be sad."

"Maybe she'll never want to leave and go to Ohio. She likes it here."

"Anyway, changing the subject, didn't you say you have a twin?"

"*Jah,* she was busy in the kitchen this morning. She was baking bread and it was just at that stage where she couldn't leave it and that's why she couldn't come out and say hello."

"And what stage is that?"

"Er, what do you mean?"

"At what stage can't the bread be left?"

Daisy scratched her neck. "Just when it's being kneaded. She had flour up to her elbows." Daisy felt bad and decided never again to tell him even one little lie. She'd thought nothing of telling him something that wasn't exactly true, but then she had to tell a bigger lie to cover up the first one.

"I see. I'll meet her another time, then. Perhaps at the Sunday meeting."

"*Jah.*"

Soon they were driving by the river where there were local craft shops and fresh-produce markets.

"Do you like pretzels?" Daisy asked.

"I do."

"I bet you've never had pretzels like the ones they make here."

"I can't wait to try them. I hope they're as good as you say."

"Stop the buggy over there," Daisy directed as she pointed to another buggy that was parked nearby.

Once they were out on the sidewalk, Daisy looked up at him and smiled. "Follow me." She showed him the town, taking him from one store to another.

"Now I've seen the stores, what else can you show me?"

She frowned at him. "We've still got a lot more of them to see."

He sighed. "Lead on."

Daisy hoped that they'd be together until nightfall. "Do you have to be back at any particular time?"

"*Nee,* I've got all day." He turned to her and smiled. "Valerie's hoping you'll convince me to stay on."

"I'll do my best. I'd like you to stay here too. What kind of things do you like?"

"Food."

"Everyone likes food."

"We haven't even had a pretzel yet."

Daisy laughed at him. "You're a typical man."

"Am I?"

"*Jah,* you are. As soon as we've finished looking through one more store, we can have something to eat."

"*Gut.* Something to look forward to."

Daisy giggled, hoping she wasn't laughing too much.

She didn't want him to think she was a giggling silly girl. She wanted him to think of her as a woman worth marrying. She knew he was putting on an act, and that he really didn't mind shopping with her. "Let's have a look in the candy store."

"If I have to."

"*Jah,* you do." When they walked into the candy store, Daisy saw Nathanial Schumacher at the rear of the store. "I just remembered candy's bad for you. Let's go."

"*Nee,* if you don't mind waiting a moment, I'll take Valerie back some caramel fudge. It's her favorite."

"Okay." Daisy was stuck there so she turned aside, hoping Nathanial wouldn't see her. She turned and pretended to look at something on the shelves at the side of the store.

"Hello, Daisy, or is it Lily?"

It was too late. She hesitated and when she turned around, she noticed that Bruno was staring at her and then he looked over at Nathanial. Daisy had no choice but to respond to Nathanial, who had the worst timing in the world.

CHAPTER 7

"Oh, hello, Nathanial. I'm Daisy. What are you doing back here?"

Nathanial took his eyes from her and glanced at Bruno, who had moved to stand next to her. "I'm back doing some work, helping my *onkel.*"

"The *onkel* who makes the buggies?" she asked.

"That's right." He offered his hand to Bruno. "Hello, I'm Nathanial Schumacher."

Bruno leaned forward and shook his hand. "I'm Bruno Weber."

She had to act normal; she didn't want Bruno to know there had been anything between herself and Nathanial. "Bruno is visiting from Ohio."

"Really? I'm from Ohio too. From the edge of Ohio."

The two men chatted on about their geographical locations while Daisy just wanted to run away. Nathanial was the last person that she wanted to see.

"And you two are just out shopping, are you?" Nathanial asked.

Bruno answered, "Daisy is being kind enough to show me around."

"Bruno is Valerie Miller's *bruder*. Have you ever met her?"

"I can't say that I have. I don't know everyone, though."

"You come here quite a bit, do you?" Bruno asked Nathanial.

"I haven't been here for a couple of years now after a particularly nasty upheaval I had with someone in the community, but I won't go into that now." He smiled and looked directly at Daisy.

Daisy put her fingertips up to her face and cleared her throat. He was hinting, hoping Bruno would ask what he was talking about. It was the incident they'd had when Nathanial had taken her on a buggy ride. She was surprised he had the nerve to come back into the area and, even worse, to make reference to what happened.

"That's too bad," Bruno said. "I'm staying with my *schweschder* because her husband's just died."

"Ah, I'm sorry to hear that."

"I'm doing my best to make her see that she should come back home with me for good. She's all alone here now."

Daisy said, "She's not alone, Bruno. She's got so many friends in the community."

Bruno nodded. "You keep telling me that. Maybe I'll feel better when I see the evidence with my own eyes. I should stick around. Well, I will be until I know she's going to be okay."

"Daisy could be right. It takes a while to heal after

someone has died. My *vadder* died not too long ago," Nathanial said.

"I didn't know that," Daisy said, suddenly seeing the softer side of him. "Your *vadder* would be Mark and Matthew's *onkel?*"

He nodded. "That's right. Mark and Rose were there at his funeral."

"I didn't even know they'd gone to Ohio." Since Rose had married, Daisy wasn't as close with her. In fact, she hardly ever saw her. "I guess I'm not as close to her as I once was."

"Daisy's older *schweschder,* Rose, is married to my cousin, Mark," Nathanial explained to Bruno.

"I guessed from the conversation that might have been the case," Bruno said. "If you two will excuse me, I'll look for some caramel fudge for Valerie. I think I can see some over there." He pointed to the other side of the store.

Daisy had no choice but to be alone with Nathanial. "What are you really doing here, Nathanial?"

"That's not a very nice way to speak to someone, especially for a deacon's *dochder.*"

Daisy shook her head, thinking that he should be pleased that she was speaking to him at all.

He stepped closer and whispered, "You've ruined my reputation and nearly ruined my life with the lies you told everyone about me."

"I didn't tell any lies; you attacked me."

"I didn't attack you." He turned to make sure no one could hear them. He stared back at her, and whispered, "I thought you wanted me to kiss you. I'd kissed girls before and that's how it always started out. You wanted me to kiss you and as soon as I tried, you jumped out of the buggy. Then you went around telling everyone I attacked you."

"Don't be ridiculous," she hissed in a low tone before she glanced over at Bruno, hoping he'd heard none of the conversation.

Nathanial continued, "No one would believe me. There was no point trying to defend myself against your lies. One thing my *vadder* always said is that the truth always comes out eventually. I might act aggressively and say mean things, but I would never attack a woman—never. Neither would I attack anyone—male or female."

"Don't try to make me believe you're in the right."

"It seems we have a different interpretation of what happened. I believe I'm right and you believe you're right."

"If you see it like that, let's just leave it at that and not talk to each other again," she said.

He smiled wickedly. "That might make things a bit awkward since I'm here for the next six months."

Daisy tilted her chin high. "It won't be awkward at all. If I see you coming, I'm just going to walk the other way."

"And what do you think your boyfriend would think about what you have to say?"

Out of the corner of her eye, she could see Bruno heading back toward them. "Don't you dare say a thing," she whispered.

"I managed to find some," Bruno said when he joined them again with the fudge in his hands. "Would you like any candy, Daisy, before I take this to the register?"

Daisy shook her head. *"Nee, denke.* I'm fine."

"She's sweet enough, it seems," Nathanial said, which made Daisy sick to her stomach.

Bruno just stared at Nathanial as though he was trying to figure him out.

Suddenly, Nathanial said, "Have you two had lunch? If you haven't, I'll take you both out for lunch—my treat. There's a place close by that I used to go to."

"I'm sorry, Nathanial. *Denke*, but Daisy and I have already made plans."

Daisy was relieved to hear Bruno's words and they made her fall more in love with him. He'd saved her from embarrassment. She wasn't going to be pushed around by Nathanial. Bruno was proving to be her perfect man. She looked at Nathanial to see how he took the refusal.

Nathanial looked annoyed. "Some other time, then. I'm sure I'll be seeing more of you, Bruno."

"I'd say so." He glanced over at Daisy. "And there might be other reasons for me to stay longer, other than my *schweschder's* well-being."

Daisy looked into Bruno's dark amber eyes and couldn't help but smile. She knew them looking at each other like that would enrage Nathanial further, but she couldn't help it—she hadn't planned to upset him.

"Another time?" Nathanial asked.

Bruno nodded. "Another time. Are you ready to go, Daisy?" Before they walked away, Bruno looked back at Nathanial, and said, "It was nice to meet you, Nathanial."

"I'll see you around, and you too, Daisy."

Daisy gave him a polite nod before she headed to the counter with Bruno to pay for the candy.

Once they were clear of the store, Daisy said, "I'm so glad you didn't take up his offer to eat with him."

"I've got you all to myself today and I'm not about to share you with another man. Besides that, I got the idea that something was wrong with him, like he didn't like seeing us together. Do you two have some kind of history? He seemed jealous to see me with you."

Daisy shook her head. "He was here a while back and I think he liked my older sister, Tulip, but she married someone else. He could be still upset about that." Remembering she wanted to be more truthful, she added, "He took me on one buggy ride, but I didn't like how he treated me."

"Ah." He nodded. "It's obvious he still likes you. Are you sure he's not my competition to win your heart?"

Daisy giggled at him being so forthright. *"Nee,* not at all. He would be the last man I would be interested in. Anyway, let's not ruin the day by talking about him any further."

By now, Daisy knew without a doubt that Bruno liked her as much as she liked him. He'd as good as said so.

"That suits me just fine. Where are we going to eat?"

"I know a nice place." Daisy walked with him to the restaurant, glad that he dropped the subject of Nathanial so quickly, but something told her that Nathanial wasn't going to stop giving her a hard time. He seemed to have a chip on his shoulder as far as she was concerned.

CHAPTER 8

*D*aisy wasn't hungry and her stomach churned. It had been awful running into Nathanial unexpectedly like that. She tried to ignore her irritation over the man. Instead, she'd turn her attention into making sure that Bruno saw that she'd make a wonderful wife for him.

"What shall we have?" He picked up the menu.

Even though she wasn't hungry, she'd have to force something down so Bruno wouldn't realize she was so distressed and upset over seeing Nathanial.

"I'll have the potato pie. I had it here once before and it was *wunderbaar,*" she said.

"Potato pie it is." He closed the menu and smiled at her. "You have the most incredible eyes, Daisy."

Daisy giggled. "They are just plain brown eyes."

"There's nothing plain about them; they're beautiful."

"Stop it! You're making me blush."

"I haven't said half of the things I'm thinking."

She touched the front of her prayer *kapp* to smooth down her hair. "Go on, tell me. What are you thinking?"

"Do you really want to know?"

"*Jah*, I do."

"You have the perfect shaped face; you're as beautiful as an angel. Are you an angel?"

Daisy giggled. "You're being silly. Anyway, all the angels in the Bible were men, weren't they?"

He laughed. "I guess that's true, but when I think of an angel, I think of a beautiful woman."

"There was Gabriel, and I can't think of any others. I don't think they all had names."

"I think you're right; that's the only name I can remember, too. Oh wait, I think there was also Michael."

They stared into each other's eyes.

"We have to order at the counter." Daisy stood up to put their orders in.

He reached out and grabbed her hand. "I'm paying for it, Daisy. This is my treat. No angel has ever paid for her own meal." Slowly, he released her hand.

Daisy sat down, now well and truly embarrassed. She felt her cheeks grow hot and she knew her face had turned bright red. This man was an answer to her prayers; he was everything she'd dreamed of except for the part about not being a twin. Had God gone to sleep when she'd added the part about how the man she loved would have to be a twin so her sister could marry his twin brother?

She fanned the menu against her face in an effort to cool it down while she watched Bruno leaning against the counter. He was tall and muscular, but he wasn't spectacularly attractive facially—his beautiful eyes and warm smile melted her heart just the same.

After he'd ordered the food, he sat back down and she placed the menu back on the table.

"How's your *schweschder* doing? It must be a comfort to her to have you visiting her. She must be devastated about losing Dirk. Dirk wasn't really that old and everyone's a little surprised that he died in the way that he did."

"Why? Has there been talk?"

"I hate to say it." Daisy pulled a face. "There has been a little bit of talk that he might have killed himself. Don't say anything to Valerie, though. She'd be upset enough without hearing that."

His gaze fell to the table. "I would never tell her anything like that. I wouldn't want to add to her grief."

"I guess it's something that will take a long time to get over."

"Maybe it's something that people never get over; they just learn to live with it."

She shook her head. "I think my mother wouldn't want to live if something happened to my father. You should see the way that they look at each other. I'm sure they're just as much in love as the day they married."

"That's nice. It would be nice if all marriages were like that."

"You don't think they are?" Daisy asked.

"*Nee*, they're not. I know for a fact that they're not."

"That's sad."

"That's life, I guess."

"Have you ever come close to being married?" Daisy asked.

"A couple of years back now."

Daisy was truly shocked. She'd expected a completely different answer. "Why didn't you go through with it?"

"I got very close. It was two weeks before the wedding and I called everything off."

Daisy was surprised. The same thing happened to Tulip. Wilhem, the man she had married, had also called off a wedding a couple of weeks before it had been due to take place. It had probably taken courage for him to call off a wedding, but at the same time, it made her feel uneasy. Perhaps he was a man who didn't know his own mind. "The girl must have been very upset."

"Yeah, she was. So upset she got married four months later to a friend of mine."

Suddenly finding herself laughing, Daisy felt much better. "I'm sorry, maybe I shouldn't laugh? I'm glad she found someone else, though. I wouldn't have wanted her to be upset. And are they both happy now?"

"They seem to be, but who really knows unless you're living in their home?"

"I suppose that's true. My two older brothers and my two older sisters are all married and they are really happy."

"Same with all my sisters. They're all married. So far, I've been happy not being married."

"Is your mother trying to marry you off?"

He laughed and seemed a little embarrassed. "How did you know that? Did Valerie say something?"

"*Nee,* she didn't. I just guessed from something you said before. Now I know that all your sisters are married, and I guessed your parents want you to marry soon. You'll have to carry on the family name because you're the only son."

"You're right. That's one of the reasons I was glad to get away and come here. There's a girl from home and she's got it into her mind that I should marry her. Mind you, she's had a little bit of help from my *mudder*. I've been sure to give her no encouragement at all."

"That's terrible. No wonder you're hiding at Valerie's place."

"That's just an added benefit of being here. The main reason is to make sure Valerie's okay."

"I understand. I was only joking."

The waiter brought their potato pies to the table along with a glass pitcher of orange juice.

"I forgot to ask what you wanted to drink. Is fresh orange juice okay?"

"*Jah*, that's good." Daisy was pleased that she was getting to know more about him. He was very open about himself, which Daisy liked.

When they were halfway through their pies, he said, "I might as well get this over now. I hope you and I can do something another day. Would you allow me to take you out again?"

Daisy swallowed the mouthful she was chewing. "I'd like that."

"Me too."

"Does that mean you want to go back to Valerie soon? Are we running out of time?"

He shook his head. "*Nee*, I've got all the time in the world. I think my *schweschder* will appreciate some time by herself."

"That's good. I've still got so many things to show you. I found it hard to know what to say to her yesterday. I didn't know whether to avoid talking about Dirk or not because I didn't want to make her cry. In the end, she did cry."

"Crying is unavoidable, I'm afraid, at times like these. She's got a lot of adjusting to do. This will be a new stage of her life. I'm doing all I can to make it easier for her."

"And that's why you want her to go back with you?"

"That's right." He popped another portion of pie into his mouth.

"That might be too many changes at the one time."

He swallowed. "I know, but at least I'll be there to keep an eye on her."

"I can keep an eye on her, along with the rest of my family."

"*Denke*, that's kind, and I know Valerie has got a lot of friends here, but is that the same as family?"

Daisy thought about her own family and how she'd feel if they weren't around. "I can't really say. I've grown up with always having Lily around. She's always gone everywhere with me except for the last few weeks."

"What's been different about the last few weeks?" He leaned forward, placing his chin on his knuckles after placing his elbow on the table.

Had she said too much? She moved what was left of her pie around her plate with her fork. "As you know, I live at home and help my *mudder* with her duties as well as the household duties."

"She does a lot of things for the community, doesn't she?"

"That's right. She's had so much work on that these days she sends Lily and I on separate errands." Looking up at him, she hoped that what she'd said didn't make her sound as though she was too young for him. Would he want to marry someone who still did errands for their mother? Or would he want a woman who worked and was industrious and had already saved money for her future family's life? At that moment, she realized she hadn't planned for her future. She'd been lazy and that couldn't be attractive to a man like Bruno. Her older sisters, Tulip and Rose, both had jobs long before they'd gotten married.

"That must keep you very busy, helping your *mudder*."

"It really does. Too busy to get a job like my older sisters."

He leaned back in his chair. "And what kind of work would you like to do if you had to get a job?"

"I don't know. I'd do anything really. I'm a fast learner."

"I had many different jobs until I settled into what I'm doing now." He stretched out his hand, took hold of his glass, and drained the last of his orange juice.

"What kind of things did you do?" She took another sip of juice.

He placed his empty glass back onto the table. "I did all sorts of things. I was a cleaner, a laborer, I did anything and everything to get money together."

"And now you're happy and settled in what you're doing?"

"*Jah*, I am."

"That's not good."

He frowned and his mouth tilted to one side. "It's not?"

"Nee. I'm helping Valerie talk you into moving here. If you weren't happy in your job, it'd be easy to have you move here." She giggled.

He laughed. "Two against one?"

"I'm sure you'd like it here."

"Maybe I like it here already." He stared into her eyes so much that she had to look away. "I'm sorry. I didn't mean to embarrass you."

"You didn't." She looked back at him. "Maybe you did a little."

He gave her a big smile. "Are you ready?"

"Jah, I'll take you somewhere special."

"Can't wait."

CHAPTER 9

*D*aisy stopped at the front of the house after Bruno had taken her home. She waited until he was out of sight and then ran into the house to find Lily. The first person she saw was her mother, who was sitting on the couch in the living room darning socks.

"There you are. You're just in time to help with the dinner. Join your *schweschder* in the kitchen."

"Okay."

"Wait!"

Daisy swung around to face her mother. *"Jah?"*

"Did you have a good time?"

"I did."

"Help Lily now and you can tell us all about it over dinner."

The last thing she wanted to do was tell her parents how things had gone with Bruno. Their outing had felt like a date and she didn't want to tell her parents what happened on her date. It was private.

Lily's face was beaming when Daisy saw her sitting at

the kitchen table shelling peas. "I saw him just now and also earlier when he collected you."

"And? What do you think of him?"

"He looked handsome from a distance, but that's not really important. Not to me it isn't, anyway."

"Me either. Of course it isn't." She sat down next to Lily and helped with the peas. "We had a really good time and he wants to see me again."

"I'm happy for you. It's just that he doesn't live around here."

"He could move. Valerie moved for love."

"So, tell me all about your day. What's he like?"

"The only way I can describe him is that he's wonderful, because that's what he is. And before I tell you more, I must tell you that Nathanial is back."

"What do you mean he's back? Back in town?"

Daisy nodded. "I was showing Bruno all the stores by the river and Nathanial was in the candy store. I turned to leave, but Bruno said he wanted to get candy for Valerie. Nathanial walked up to us and ..."

"What did you do?"

Daisy licked her lips. "It wasn't easy. I had to make like we had no qualms with each other. I introduced Bruno to Nathanial as though he was just someone normal because that was all I could do. I didn't want Bruno to think there was something strange going on. I couldn't tell him about what Nathanial did."

"That would've been hard to just act like nothing was wrong."

"It was. And after I introduced the two of them, Nathanial asked Bruno and me to go to lunch with him.

What do you think about that? He was trying to torture me."

"Oh no! How did you get out of it?"

"Bruno jumped in and said we had plans."

"That was good. He must've wanted to be alone with you." Lily shook her head. "That would be just like Nathanial to want to make you feel uncomfortable. I wonder what he's doing back here. Doesn't he know he's not wanted around these parts? I'm shocked that he showed his face. Do you think you should tell *Dat?*"

"*Nee.* Word will get out that he's here. If he's not sent away when he turns up at the Sunday meeting, there'll be nothing we can do about it. He blames me for everything and for having to leave last time. Soon after Nathanial was talking to both of us, Bruno decided to get his sister some candy and left the two of us alone."

Lily leaned forward. "Did you tell him to go away and leave you alone?"

"I didn't want to be that rude, but anyway, he blamed me for everything that happened between us. He said that I wanted to be kissed and many girls before me had been kissed and I had no reason to jump out of the buggy and run away."

Lily shook her head. "He's kissed lots of girls? That's just awful, Daisy. Do you think it's true? Maybe it's not. He could've just said that because he was mad."

"Does it matter?"

"Well, is that all he did? He only tried to kiss you? That doesn't sound that bad. You could've just said you didn't want to kiss him, rather than run away."

"You weren't there. Trust me, it wasn't good. It wasn't

like he said, not at all. Anyway, I don't want to talk about him."

"Tell me more about Bruno."

"The rest of the day with Bruno was amazing." Daisy couldn't stop smiling. "He's just perfect; he's just the perfect man for me. He must've known I didn't want to have lunch with Nathanial and he told him we had other plans just like a real man would've said. Bruno stood up to him without being rude."

"Bruno looks a bit older than you."

"*Jah.* I don't know how old exactly, but I know he's quite a bit older. Do you think that matters?" Daisy didn't mind one little bit how old he was. Besides, he wasn't that old—not too old for her at all. This man was a great match for her and she knew it.

"There is that saying that if something looks too perfect, maybe it is."

Daisy frowned. "What do you mean?

"If he's so great, why hasn't he married before now?"

"He's never met anybody that he wanted to marry. Actually, he told me he came close a while ago and stopped before things went too far. Also, there's a woman who everyone wants him to marry and that's another reason he's here looking after Valerie."

Lily gasped and covered her mouth.

"What is it?" Daisy asked.

"What if he's doing what Jacob did to Rose? He could have been involved with that woman in the way that he shouldn't have been, and then he's run away and you're his next victim?"

Daisy narrowed her eyes at her sister. Why was she

saying horrible things about Bruno? Didn't she want her to be happy? "Do you think he's been involved intimately with this woman he's left behind?"

"I wouldn't say something like that, but if something seems too good to be true, maybe it is, and maybe he's not as perfect as he appears to be. Don't rush into anything. 'Marry in haste, repent at leisure.'"

Daisy arched an eyebrow. "Are you just saying this because he's not a twin?"

"*Nee.* Rose was fooled by Jacob, remember?"

"Of course I do. Something like that is hard to forget. Poor Rose was so upset."

"And do you want to be fooled in just the same way?"

"Of course I don't, but I don't think he's like that. He's a really good man."

"Why don't you get *Dat* to ask questions about him just to be sure? You think he's perfect, but Rose thought Jacob was before she married Mark, and then you also thought Nathanial was perfect once."

"*Nee*, I won't do that. I won't have *Dat* thinking something is wrong with Bruno because I would know—I would know in my heart."

"If you think so. I'm only trying to help."

"I know you are. I'm just sad that he doesn't have any brothers."

Lily giggled. "That was just a childish thing for us to think, Daisy. It was nice to think that we could live together forever, but we could live nearby each other and visit every day."

"*Jah*, we'll have to do that. We can't be separated too much, or I'd die."

Lily giggled. "Me too. I think you'll end up getting married to Bruno and I will meet someone at your wedding—maybe Bruno's cousin, if he has one."

Their mother walked into the kitchen and looked at the pile of peas in the container. "Is there any work going on in here or just a lot of talk?"

"We're working too, *Mamm*," Daisy answered.

LATER THAT NIGHT, Daisy was in her room with Lily just before bedtime. Daisy pulled her long dark hair over one shoulder. She began to braid her hair, as was her nightly routine, into one long braid.

"Turn around. I'll do your hair."

Daisy turned around, flipping her hair over her back, pleased that she'd told Lily everything about Bruno. She would be careful, as Lily suggested. Being impulsive had never led her anywhere good in the past.

"I hope Nathanial doesn't try to ruin things with Bruno and you. Do you think he was jealous?" Lily asked.

"*Nee*. What happened was so long ago. He wouldn't have even given it two thoughts. Hopefully he's matured since then." His words at the candy store had shown otherwise, but Daisy pushed that out of her mind, preferring not to let anything ruin her good mood.

When Lily went into her own room, her words of earlier that day about Bruno not being perfect swirled in Daisy's head. She slipped between the covers of her bed and went over the day she'd had with Bruno. He seemed so perfect, but was she just setting herself up for a fall? She'd also liked Nathanial before she'd gone on that disastrous buggy ride with him a long time ago. What if Bruno was simply putting on a good act?

Daisy decided to be guarded just in case. She would not give her heart away too soon. He'd run from a woman in Ohio, so what if he was someone who ran when a relationship got serious? It was quite possible that it was so.

CHAPTER 10

*W*hen Nancy and Hezekiah were getting ready for bed, Nancy asked, "What do you think of Valerie's *bruder,* Bruno?"

"He seems a man of good reputation from what I've heard so far. Do you want me to ask further about him?"

"Jah, I think that would be a good idea. You know what the twins are like—they don't have much sense about men or anything else."

"You don't trust them?"

"Nee. I don't trust them to make good decisions. I think they've proven that they don't always know how to make decisions."

"Valerie's *familye* is *gut.* I know that, but I'll keep asking. I don't think we've got anything to worry about there."

"Gut. See what you can find out, would you?"

"Of course I will. Daisy's already spent the day with him."

"Still, I'd like you to ask about him. I can tell she likes him. Why don't I ask him over for dinner with Valerie?"

"Okay. When?"

"I'll ask them at the Sunday meeting if they'll come for dinner on the following Monday."

"Fine by me," he said.

"Okay. I meant to have Valerie over soon anyway. She wants to talk with me about doing volunteer work."

"It works out good all around then."

"*Jah.*"

"Daisy seems quite serious about Bruno," he said.

"She can't be too serious about him; she's only just met him."

Hezekiah shrugged his shoulders. "Seems like it to me, though. She kept smiling throughout dinner and did you notice when we asked her about her day she deliberately didn't talk about him?"

"Now that you mention it, I can see that she didn't like to tell us much about him. Sounds like she wants to keep things to herself."

"Or not say his name in front of me," Hezekiah said. "*Vadders* are always the last to know anything."

Nancy giggled. "And *mudders* too. We'll have to see what Bruno's like when he's here for dinner."

"What you won't be pleased to hear is that Nathanial Schumacher is back here, staying for a few months while he's helping his *onkel.*"

"That's dreadful. When did he get here? Couldn't you have kept him away?"

"I can't do that."

"You could've told the bishop exactly what he did to Daisy."

"I said enough and besides, we don't know what he did to Daisy." He scratched his neck. "I don't like to say it, but …"

"You think she made the whole thing up?"

"*Nee*, I'm not saying that, but …"

"You think she might have exaggerated what happened?"

He grimaced. "*Jah*, I think it's possible. I didn't want to say anything to you about it before now. At the time, I was enraged with Nathanial, but when everything calmed down, I got to thinking what Daisy's like and … let's just say I have a question mark there."

Part of her wanted to be upset with her husband for thinking such a thing, but she'd had the same thoughts cross her mind too. Then again, he was Jacob's brother. "I think he's just like his older *bruder*, Jacob. They're bad seeds."

"You can't judge someone by their siblings. Every man has to stand on his own and be judged by his own works. *Gott* knows every man's heart and He's the judge."

"But meanwhile, we have to keep our *dochders* safe and away from men like Nathanial. We just can't take the risk."

"I agree, but at the same time, I can't point the finger at him and say he's done something when we don't have details and Daisy won't talk about it."

"She's embarrassed."

"I know, but she won't even tell you the full account of what happened that night, so it's hard for me to say anything to the bishop when I don't know the full story."

"She's said enough."

"Still, I don't have any reason to ask him to leave, and neither can I say anything to the bishop to cause him to ask Nathanial to leave. When it happened, I hinted to the bishop and he took note."

"He must be guilty. He left the community quickly when it all happened."

"I don't think he'll give Daisy any more trouble. Daisy seems fond of Bruno, so let's just leave things be. I'll keep an eye on Nathanial."

"Okay. I'll put Nathanial Schumacher out of my mind, and I'll invite Valerie and Bruno for dinner Monday night if they haven't made other plans."

Hezekiah smiled at his wife, leaned over, and kissed her on her cheek.

CHAPTER 11

*D*aisy was pleased to be going to the Sunday meeting because she knew she would see Bruno again. But ... she hoped Nathanial wasn't planning on causing trouble between herself and Bruno. It had been obvious that Bruno and she liked each other as more than just friends, and that had irritated Nathanial—she could see it on his face.

The meeting that Sunday was held at the Stoltzfus' house, old Mary's eldest son's place. Daisy sat down at the back of the living room next to Lily. They had both walked past Nathanial and he had smiled at them, but Daisy had looked the other way as soon as he'd done so. She hadn't meant to be rude; she was nervous and didn't want to give him any encouragement. Just before the meeting began, Valerie and Bruno walked in and took their seats. Before Bruno sat down, Daisy noticed he quickly looked around the room and saw where she was.

Lily leaned in close. "That's him, isn't it?"

"*Jah*, what do you think?"

"He seems all right, but he's not my type."

Daisy glared at her sister. They'd always had the same taste in everything so why wouldn't they have the same taste in men? "Why isn't he your type?"

"I don't know; he's kind of—too old or something."

"He's not that much older than us. Anyway, he mightn't be super handsome, but he doesn't need to be. He's perfect on the inside and that suits me just fine."

"That's all that matters," Lily said.

It had surprised Daisy that Lily hadn't been very encouraging.

"I hope Nathanial is not going to stay around too long," Lily whispered and then added, "Didn't you say he was working for his *onkel* for a few weeks?"

"*Jah,* but I was just hoping he would go sooner."

"Don't let it bother you, Daisy."

"I'll try not to."

Their mother, who was sitting directly in front of them, turned around and shot them a heated glare for whispering.

They kept quiet the rest of the meeting.

WHEN THE MEAL WAS SERVED, after the meeting was over, it was the twins' time to socialize.

All Daisy wanted to do was run over and talk to Bruno immediately, but she didn't want tongues to wag, so she restrained herself. Every now and again when she was talking to people, she would see Bruno looking in her direction.

Halfway through the meal, she saw her mother and

father talking to Bruno. She dug her sister in the ribs. "Look, Lily. I don't like the look of that."

"Why not? They're just being friendly with him since he's a visitor to the community."

"*Nee*, there's more to it than that. I should never have told *Mamm* about liking Bruno. Remember how pushy she was when she was trying to get Rose and Tulip married off?"

"*Mamm* would never be like that with us. She knows how sensible we both are."

"*Jah*, that's true," Daisy said with a giggle.

Lily said, "Do you want me to go over and see if I can hear what they're saying?"

"*Nee*. I'll go over and speak with him when they go. He'll tell me what they said."

"I'm sure there's nothing to worry about."

When her mother and father had finished speaking with Bruno, she casually walked over to him.

"How are you, Daisy? I was wondering when you were going to come and speak with me."

"Well, you could've come to me." Daisy laughed.

"I wasn't sure you'd want me to—only because people might talk."

"There's nothing we can do to prevent that happening. I'm not worried about that."

"That's good. If I'd known that, I would've been straight over to see you as soon as the meeting finished."

"I just noticed my parents were speaking with you."

"*Jah*, they invited me and Valerie to dinner."

Daisy was speechless. "Why did they … I mean …"

He laughed and touched her arm lightly. "I was a little surprised too, but pleased about it."

"When—when are you coming for dinner?"

"Tomorrow night."

Daisy was delighted that her mother was helping her with her new romance. That meant her mother and father approved of him. She already knew they liked Valerie a lot, and they must've liked Bruno just as much.

"I'll look forward to you coming. Did she say there would be anyone else there besides you and Valerie?" Daisy wondered whether her mother would be inviting the whole family—her brothers and their wives, and her two older sisters and their husbands.

He shook his head. "She didn't say. It'll be good to get to know your parents better. They seem nice, just like my parents."

CHAPTER 12

*W*hen Daisy woke up, she immediately remembered that Bruno was coming to dinner. This would be the first time that Lily would meet him, since they hadn't spoken at the Sunday meeting. She'd already worked out the dinner menu with her mother the night before. They were having roast chicken with bread stuffing, mashed potatoes, and coleslaw, and for dessert they were having fruit salad and tapioca pudding. She'd told her mother that she would do most of the cooking.

Her stomach churned at the thought of seeing Bruno again. She changed out of her nightdress, pulling on a clean dress. She wasted no time on her hair, figuring she'd fix it before Bruno arrived—for now she tucked her long braid under her prayer *kapp*. When she was done dressing, she headed downstairs.

"There you are," her mother said when she walked into the kitchen. "I let you sleep in and I was just about to wake you."

"Did I sleep in?" Daisy looked out the window to see a gray overcast sky. She always slept in when the sky was gray like that. "I didn't mean to."

"Never mind. I had to send Lily to the store without you. There were a few things I needed."

"I could've gone with her."

"There's no use sending the two of you to do a job that only takes one. Now fix yourself some breakfast and then we'll start cleaning this *haus* from top to bottom. I don't want Valerie to think we live in a dirty place."

"The *haus* is already clean."

Her mother's face soured. "Not to my standards."

"What do you want me to do first?"

"Have something to eat and then we can start on the floors. After the floors are washed, it'll have to be the windows. We'll start the cooking at three."

"Okay."

When her mother went out of the room, Daisy fixed herself some eggs. She was a little disappointed to miss out on going to the store with Lily, but Bruno coming there tonight more than made up for it.

It was two o'clock in the afternoon and Lily still hadn't come home.

"I should go and look for her, *Mamm*."

"She should've been home hours ago."

Daisy nibbled on the end of her fingernail. "I hope she hasn't had an accident or something."

"She'll want to have had an accident if she comes home

this late. Otherwise, she'll have no *gut* excuse for getting out of chores."

"I'm certain she'll have a reason. Let me go and look for her."

Her mother nodded. "Okay, but don't take too long."

When Daisy was halfway to the barn, she saw Lily coming up the driveway in the buggy pulled by their bay gelding.

She hurried toward her. "Where have you been, Lily?"

"Am I late or something?"

"*Jah*, and *Mamm's* furious."

"I lost track of the time. That's all."

"You better think of some reason why you were gone so long. You know how she likes to scrub the *haus* extra well before people come for dinner."

"How mad is she?"

"Very. You go and see her and I'll rub the horse down for you and unhitch the buggy."

"*Denke*, Daisy."

Lily jumped out of the buggy and, with the groceries in her arms, walked slowly to the house. Before she reached the door, it was flung open and their mother stood there scowling at Lily with her arms folded tightly across her chest.

When Daisy led the horse into the barn, she could hear her mother berating her sister. She did everything as quickly as she could so she could get back to the house.

Once she got back and entered the kitchen, Lily was nowhere to be seen. Her mother was mixing the bread stuffing for the chicken with her fingers.

"Where's Lily?"

"I sent her up to her room."

That meant Lily was in big trouble. "Can I go and see her?"

"Nee, you can't. You'll help me here."

Her mother was in one of those moods where she was not to be crossed.

Half an hour later, her mother disappeared from the kitchen and Daisy guessed she'd gone to see Lily. It wouldn't be nice if Bruno and his sister came to the house and sensed the tension. She hoped Lily and their mother would work things out right now.

Lily came down the stairs five minutes later with her mother walking close behind her. Lily was given the job of scrubbing the bathroom—the chore she and Daisy hated the most.

Later, when Lily and Daisy had a quiet moment, Daisy asked her why she'd been gone for so long in town.

"Like I said, I lost track of time. I looked around the stores and I stopped to have something to eat. I didn't know I was supposed to come right back as soon as I got the groceries. We normally look around the stores together."

"Jah, but tonight we've got people coming for dinner and that means scrubbing the *haus."*

"We clean it every day; it's fine."

"You and I know that, but *Mamm* doesn't."

The girls stopped talking when their mother came back into the kitchen.

"Less talk and more work, please. Our guests will be here soon and we don't want to have them waiting until late at night to be fed."

They all heard the front door open, and their mother rushed to greet their father.

"I hope she doesn't tell *Dat* that I was away so long."

"He won't mind. He'll tell *Mamm* she's fussing about things again."

Lily giggled. "She doesn't like it when he says that."

"You'll have to tell me honestly what you think of Bruno."

"Jah, of course I'll be honest. Why wouldn't I be?"

"I didn't mean that you wouldn't, but you might not tell me how you really feel about him because you know I like him so much."

"I'll be honest and tell you exactly what I think of him," Lily said as she picked up another pod of peas to shell.

CHAPTER 13

*D*aisy waited excitedly in the kitchen when she heard the buggy coming to the house. Her mother and father were in the living room and she and Lily were setting the table in the large dining room just off from the kitchen.

"What should I do?" Daisy asked Lily.

"Just wait here until they both come inside, and then go out into the living room."

Daisy nodded. "Okay. I'm so nervous I can't even think properly."

"Just relax; everything will be fine. Don't worry. You'll be all right—he obviously likes you."

"I guess so. He seems to like me."

Daisy did what her twin sister suggested; she stayed in the kitchen until she heard Bruno's voice in the living room and then she walked out to greet Bruno and his sister, Valerie.

Bruno looked handsome in his billowing white shirt paired with black pants held up by black suspenders. He'd made an effort to dress well—far different from the casual clothes he was wearing when she'd first met him at Valerie's *haus*.

"Daisy, it's nice to see you again," he said, smiling.

"Hello, Bruno. Hi, Valerie."

"Hello, Daisy. I was just telling Bruno how alike you and Lily are."

"*Jah*, they haven't met yet."

"I saw Lily yesterday at the meeting from across the yard, but I haven't spoken to her yet. It would be hard to tell the two of you apart." He turned to Mr. Yoder. "I guess you can tell which one is which?"

He laughed. "I can. I've had many years of practice. They are slightly different in the face, but even I can't tell who's who from a distance."

Right on cue, Lily walked into the room.

Daisy linked arms with Lily. "This is Lily."

"It's nice to meet you, Bruno. Hello again, Valerie."

"Hello, Lily," Valerie said.

Bruno smiled at her. "Hello, Lily. The resemblance is amazing."

Lily giggled. "I'm wearing the green dress and Daisy is wearing the purple dress."

"I'll remember that," he said.

"Dinner smells *wunderbaar*, Nancy," Valerie said.

"*Denke*. I hope it tastes as good."

Lily and Daisy sat on the couch next to Valerie, and Bruno sat on the couch opposite, next to the twins' parents.

"Why don't you go and make us some coffee, Daisy?" their mother suggested. "It'll be a little while before dinner."

"Of course." Daisy bounded to her feet.

"Shall I help?" Bruno said, standing up.

Daisy thought quickly. *"Jah,* I might need help carrying everything out."

The two of them hurried to the kitchen.

Bruno sat down at the kitchen table and watched Daisy make the coffee. "It was nice of your parents to invite us to dinner."

"They like Valerie, and it seems as though they might like you, too."

"How can you tell?'

"I can just tell."

"Do you want me to help you with anything there?"

"Nee, denke. You can help carry the tray in when everything's ready."

"I think I can manage that. When can we see each other again?"

She turned away from the stove where she'd just placed the pot to boil. She stared at him. "When would you like to do that?"

"Tomorrow?"

Daisy gave a quiet giggle. "I'll see if I can get away."

"There are a few repairs I want to make to Valerie's *haus.* I'll ask your *vadder* if you could come with me to show me the best places to buy the hardware."

"He might point out I don't know anything about hardware. Is that the best excuse you can come up with?"

"Can you think of a better one?" He smiled at her.

She shook her head. "Not quickly."

"That'll have to do, then."

She sat down at the table with him.

"Did you have any other plans for tomorrow?" he asked.

"*Nee*. Each day is pretty much the same for me. *Mamm* helps the community a lot, so she's always having us help her to either visit people or sew things that we can sell for charities."

"That's nice. It must feel good to be so useful to so many people. I know Valerie appreciates the help your *familye* has been."

"*Dat* says everyone needs a helping hand every once in a while and tomorrow it could be us."

"*Vadders* are so wise sometimes; mine says if one person in the community is hurting then we're all not well."

"Is he a part of the church oversight?"

"*Nee*, he's not. He was very strict when we were growing up. He's relaxed a little in his old age."

"What about your *mudder?*"

"She's a very kind and gentle woman—she's quietly spoken."

Lily walked into the kitchen. "Can I help with anything?"

"Are they getting thirsty?" Daisy asked, surprised to see her sister.

Lily said, "*Nee*, but they were talking about things and I thought I should make myself scarce."

"What were they talking about?" Bruno asked.

"They're talking about Valerie possibly selling the farm."

Bruno nodded. "That's something she's been wanting to talk over with someone like your *vadder*."

Lily glanced at the bare table, and then the pot on the stove. Without saying anything, she gathered the tray, cups, teaspoons, and everything else they'd need for their coffee.

"*Denke*, Lily," Daisy said, glad that one of them was thinking straight. All she could think about was Bruno and wanting to be alone with him.

When the pot boiled, Daisy made the coffee and the girls followed Bruno back out to the living room.

THAT NIGHT, when Lily and Daisy were having their usual nightly chat in Daisy's bedroom, Lily leaned close to Daisy, and said, "I hope you didn't mind me coming into the kitchen. I didn't want to disturb you. I knew you'd want to be alone with him, but it wasn't right, me sitting there while Valerie talked about selling the farm and all that."

"Of course I didn't mind. I had a few minutes alone with him and he wants us to go somewhere tomorrow."

"I know. I heard him asking *Mamm* if he could come and collect you in the morning. That's *wunderbaar*. I could tell he really likes you. He couldn't stop smiling at you. I reckon you'll marry him."

Daisy's face lit up. "Do you think so?"

"I do. Then you'll have to help find someone for me. I'm not in a hurry. I'll take my time and find someone who suits me perfectly, just like Bruno suits you."

"He does suit me, doesn't he? And it was all so unexpected. One day I didn't even know him and the next day I'm in love with him."

"Are you in love?" Lily asked.

"Jah, I truly am. I can't stop thinking about him and when I'm with him, he makes me feel so happy. I can't imagine marrying anyone but him. The only thing is I don't want to move away and he doesn't live here."

"That's easy solved. Just tell him you won't marry him unless he moves here."

"Should I be that bossy? He might not like bossy women."

"Just be yourself, and you *are* bossy." Lily giggled.

"I guess I am, and if he loves me, he will move here. It'll help that Valerie wants to stay here too."

"I thought she was selling her farm. That's what she was talking about when I escaped into the kitchen."

"Bruno said she was thinking of selling the land and keeping the house."

"Can that be done?" Lily asked.

Daisy nodded. *"Jah,* people sell off parts of their land all the time."

"It'd be nice for Valerie to have her *bruder* living close by."

"Jah, it must be hard for her with her husband gone."

Lily agreed. "Especially with all that talk going around about him. I wonder if she knows what people are saying."

"I don't think she would," Daisy said.

"What do you think happened to Dirk?"

Daisy shook her head. "He's gone. That's all I know. The rest doesn't make any difference."

CHAPTER 14

*W*hen he collected Daisy the next morning, Bruno said he'd do his errands another day. Today, Daisy could take him on a tour of the local countryside and show him all her favorite spots.

Daisy had proceeded to show Bruno all the places around the area that she could think of and, even though the day was cold, he thought it would be nice to have a walk down by the river on one of the many walking trails she'd mentioned. She hoped he might be romantic and hold her hand when no one was about.

She wanted nothing more than to marry him and be happy like her sisters were. Then she could really start her life and have her own home with her own children. It had been a childish fantasy that she would marry a twin so Lily and she could be together; she knew that now.

"Shall we park the buggy here?" he asked when they drew close to the river.

"Jah, this is perfect."

They got out of the buggy and then walked side-by-side down to the riverbank. It was a little muddy and Daisy was careful where she put her feet, so she didn't slip. Soon she heard the gurgling fast-running water of the river.

"Are you warm enough?" He glanced over at her.

She pulled her black shawl tighter around her shoulders to keep out the cool breeze coming up from the water. "I'm okay." As soon as she'd spoken those words, she regretted them. If she'd said she was cold then perhaps he would've placed his coat around her shoulders, or he might have put his arm around her to keep her warm. She'd think quicker next time.

When they were on the path parallel to the river, it was more level and solid underfoot.

"It's beautiful here," he said, staring out at the river.

"It's running fast today because we've had rain lately."

He sniffed the air. "I can smell wildflowers, or something."

"It could be. There are a few around, but not for long."

They walked on in silence for quite a while.

"Are you all right? You seem a little quieter today," Daisy said.

"I've got a lot on my mind."

"Like what?" Remembering her manners, she added, "Do you want to talk about it?"

"My *mudder* wants me to go home and I've still got a lot of things to organize for Valerie."

"Why? Like what?"

"Why does she want me home or what do I have to do for Valerie?"

"Both."

"Valerie has decided to go ahead with selling off most of her land. It's a bit of a nightmare and I don't think she's in any state to do all that alone. She'll keep the *haus* and a little land, enough to have a small garden and chickens."

"That's sad that she has to sell."

"It's the best outcome. It makes sense, since she can't work the land."

"And do you want to go home, Bruno, like your *mudder* wants?"

He stopped near the water and looked across it to the other side. "*Nee*, I don't want to go home. I wouldn't be able to see you if I went home." He looked back at her.

She smiled and looked away, glad that his quiet mood had nothing to do with her.

"Why does she want you to come home?"

"It's all to do with that girl I told you about. I don't know why they're pushing her onto me. They did it once before and it ended badly. I just want to choose my own *fraa*. What's wrong with that?"

"Nothing. That's how it should be. Parents can be too pushy sometimes. Anyway, how is Valerie today?"

"She's doing okay."

"I'm sure she's grateful and pleased that you've come to help out with everything."

"I guess she is. Let's sit here and look at the river so I can take my mind off all my troubles."

Daisy gave a little giggle as they sat down on a wooden seat.

"Why does your *mudder* like this girl so much?"

"I have no idea. Maybe it's because she's available and has all the attributes of a *gut fraa*. I mean, there's nothing wrong with her, she's perfectly nice, but totally unsuited to me. There's just no spark between us. Do you know what I mean?"

Daisy smiled and nodded, and then looked over the water and wondered if he felt a 'spark' with her. She felt it with him.

They talked some more and found out more about each other, until Daisy remembered she had to be home at a reasonable hour to help her mother.

"My *familye* has a dinner every week where we all gather. It used to be about once a month, but my *mudder* changed it to once a week. It's on tonight."

"That's a lovely idea."

"That's why I have to be home early to help with the dinner."

"We'll see each other again soon, won't we?"

"I hope so."

They stood and walked back to the buggy.

"How about Friday?" he asked.

Daisy nodded. "I'd like that very much."

"Good! It's nice that your *familye* keeps close together. My parents see everyone only at the meetings and community events because they're all so busy with their own families."

"Does it feel odd to be the only one out of your siblings not married?" Daisy asked, wondering how she'd feel if Lily married first, leaving her unmarried.

"It does sometimes. I'd like nothing more than a *fraa* and a *familye* to come home to after a hard day's work." He stopped still when they reached the buggy, and then looked down into her eyes.

She smiled at him, hoping he was about to ask her to marry him. Her parents might think that they hadn't known each other long enough, but she knew that it was right. He was the man for her. Many young people in the community got married after only knowing someone for a short time.

"Daisy, I'm so glad I came to stay with Valerie. I'm so pleased to have met you."

She waited for him to keep talking, but he didn't, so she said, "I'm grateful you came because I'm happy to have met you, too."

He looked into her face for a moment before he spoke again. "Let's go. I'll take you home before it gets too late. I need to keep in good standing with your parents."

As they both climbed into the buggy, Daisy couldn't help being a little disappointed that Bruno hadn't talked about marriage. Perhaps he would take time to think about what he wanted once he got Valerie settled.

t was nice to see her brothers and sisters happily married and their families growing. Daisy's niece, Shirley, had a baby sister, Lizzie. Her older brother, Trevor, and sister-in-law, Amy, had a baby boy, now six months old, whom they had named Stephen. Rose and Mark still didn't have any children because Rose had suffered two miscarriages in the past year, which she had become depressed about.

"Rose and I have an announcement to make," Mark said, as he stood up at the table at their family dinner.

Daisy hoped that he would say that Rose was finally expecting again.

Hezekiah said, "The last time you said that, you were announcing that you and Rose were going to get married. What is it this time?"

From a standing position, Mark reached out and grabbed Rose's hand. "Rose and I are having a *boppli*."

Everyone let out delighted gasps and most people

jumped out of their seats to congratulate and kiss the happy couple.

"And it's past the danger point. I'm halfway along." Rose sat with her shoulders back and a huge grin on her face.

Daisy couldn't speak because she was so pleased. She got up and kissed Rose quickly, and then kissed Mark, before she sat down. Everything had come easy for Rose except for having a baby. Hopefully, this baby would have no problems coming into the world. She'd lost the other two early in her pregnancies. Then there was Tulip who hadn't gotten pregnant at all, and she'd been married long enough to have a baby by now. She appeared to be hiding her personal disappointment. Maybe all the Yoder girls would have problems having babies.

Daisy had been right about Tulip being upset, because Tulip and Wilhem made their excuses and left right after dessert—not even waiting for coffee in the living room.

Daisy whispered to Lily, "I think Tulip's upset that she's not had a baby and she's been married long enough."

"I thought that too, and she left early. We had best not say anything to Rose because she would get upset about Tulip being sad. Rose should be feeling happy at this time."

"Agreed," Daisy whispered back. "Anyway, I've got something to tell you later."

"About Bruno?" Lily asked.

"*Jah.*"

· · ·

AFTER THEIR GUESTS had gone home that night, Hezekiah and Nancy went up to their bedroom, leaving the twins to do the washing up and the cleaning of the kitchen.

"Rose will have our fourth *grosskin*. Isn't it wonderful news? I thought she was getting big, but I didn't say anything because I didn't want to upset her in case she wasn't expecting."

"It's certainly is good news, but I couldn't help feeling a little sorry for Tulip. Did you notice how they left early?"

"*Jah*, I did, but there's nothing we can do about that. She'll have her *boppli* soon. It took Rose some time, so it'll probably take Tulip a while too."

Nancy took off her prayer *kapp* and unpinned her hair. She ran a brush through her long hair, which ended past her thighs. Her hair had only been cut once, when she was a teenager, because the weight of it had given her headaches. It took a good twenty minutes a night to brush her hair.

When Hezekiah was changed into his pajamas, he got into bed and propped himself up with the pillows. "There's something I have to tell you, Nancy, but I don't want you to get angry or upset."

The brush slipped out of Nancy's hand and bounced across the wooden floorboards. It was not a good way for her husband to start a conversation. Her eyes fixed onto Hezekiah, wondering what was wrong. Whatever he was about to say was not going to be good. "What is it?" She held her breath, bracing herself for what was to come.

"One of the twins has been seen alone with Nathanial."

She sighed with relief, leaned down, and picked up the

brush. When she straightened up again, she said, "That was Daisy. She told me all about running into him at the candy store when she was out with Bruno."

"*Nee*, Nancy. It was Lily and they were in a café and they were holding hands. I know for certain it was Lily because Daisy was elsewhere at the time the twin was spotted."

Nancy's mouth dropped open as she stared at her husband in disbelief. "And why are you only telling me about this now?"

"I didn't want to ruin dinner."

"Better ruining my dinner than ruining Lily's life. He caused you to have a heart attack and did goodness knows what to Daisy, and now he's paying everybody back by going after Lily."

"We don't know for certain ..."

Nancy placed her brush back on the dresser and walked towards the door.

Hezekiah threw back the covers and got out of bed, getting to the door ahead of her and resting his hand on Nancy's. "Don't act in haste. No good will come of you being cross with Lily about this. This is something we have to think about more deeply." He led Nancy back to the bed and they both sat.

Nancy put her hand to her head. "I'm upset about it."

"I know, but we have to be smart about this, Nancy. Daisy told us she liked Bruno and now Lily obviously likes Nathanial, but has chosen not to tell us because she knows the fuss that happened between him and Daisy."

"I know that, Hezekiah. What are you trying to say? I want to go right in there now and ask Lily what's going on and ask her why she kept this a secret from us." Anger swirled in Nancy's head and she felt she was going to burst. She couldn't just sit there and do nothing.

"And what good would that do?"

She stared at her husband who sometimes seemed far too calm. "You want to let her sneak around behind our backs?"

"Many young people court in secret with no one looking over their shoulders."

"But he's not just any young man; he's no good."

"No one's all bad. He might have changed his ways. We don't know he hasn't transformed and repented of his ways."

"And if he hasn't? Are you willing to put our *dochder* at risk by allowing her to see more of this man who has a bad reputation?"

Hezekiah looked thoughtful and shook his head. "I don't know what to do right now. I only know that no good will come of lecturing Lily about it now. We have to be careful that we don't drive her further into his arms and away from us. I've seen things like that happen in other families."

Nancy gasped and covered her mouth with her hand. As the deacon, her husband was privy to many private matters between people in their community. "You're right; that's exactly what Lily would do. She'd run away with him. She's never really listened to what we have to say."

"Maybe the best thing we can do is to do nothing at all," Hezekiah suggested with amazing composure.

Nancy looked into her husband's eyes and was pleased

that he was so wise and level-headed. He was right about saying nothing to Lily. She'd carefully monitor the situation and step in when necessary. If Lily thought she was in love with Nathanial, she was the kind of girl who would run away with him if told she wasn't allowed to see him again. Nancy would just have to trust that she had raised Lily properly and she wouldn't do anything silly.

"We'll pray about it and have faith that *Gott* will work things out for Lily. He'll guide Lily because we will ask Him to."

Nancy nodded and put her head on her husband's shoulder. He'd always been so sensible and had a special way of calming her down and making her think first, rather than reacting to a situation. It seemed as though every time she wanted to be happy and enjoy good news, the twins had a way of doing something dreadful to ruin everything. Why couldn't they be more normal?

THEY'D HAD their family dinner and everyone had gone home, but Daisy couldn't shake the fact that Bruno had been close to talking about marriage earlier that day at the riverbank and had stopped himself. It wasn't unusual in their Amish community to have quick courtships, and young people paired together fairly quickly. Why was he so hesitant?

Lily and Daisy were having their nightly conversation in Daisy's room.

"What did I do wrong, Lily? Should I have said something different? I was certain he was going to ask me to marry him. He even talked about the girl his *mudder* is trying to make him marry and he said there was no spark with her. Surely he wouldn't have told me that unless he felt he had a spark with me, don't you think?"

"I'm not sure."

"Do you think he only sees me as a friend?"

"I don't know."

Daisy groaned. "I wish I knew what was going on in his head. Sometimes I feel I'm sure he likes me and other times I don't know if he does or not."

"Maybe you were acting too keen. Remember, he said there was that woman chasing him—the one his *mudder* wants him to marry? Perhaps you shouldn't be so keen?"

"I'm just being myself and I don't think I've been like that. I don't want to play games. I might lose him if I do. Things should happen naturally."

"Lose him? Do you reckon you have him now? If you don't have him, you can't lose him."

Daisy scrunched up her face, trying to figure out Lily's logic. "What are you talking about?"

"If he knows you'll say yes to marrying him, he loses the thrill of the chase. Men are like hunters; they like the thrill of the chase and if he knows you're keen on him, there's no thrill there."

Daisy shook her head. *"Nee,* I think you're wrong."

"Has he asked you to marry him yet?"

"Nee, you know that he hasn't."

"Well, perhaps you should play a little harder to get? That'll make him more interested. Sometimes men want what they can't have and especially a man like Bruno who's been a bachelor for some time. He's used to passing women over and in doing so, he grows more and more picky with every woman he sees as not meeting his standards."

Lily's words cut into Daisy's heart like a knife. Perhaps there was some truth in what she said. She had shown Bruno she was keen on him and although she knew that he liked her too, was that enough for him to ask her to marry him? She had to be smarter about things if she wanted Bruno as her husband.

"Lily, I think some of what you say might be true."

"I know I'm right. Just because I've never had a boyfriend doesn't mean that I don't know how these things work. If you act less keen, or if he thinks there might be someone else, he'll make sure to make you his wife. Men are territorial creatures. You don't have to say yes every time he asks you out."

"But he's only here for a short amount of time."

"He can stay longer if he wants. That's what you told me."

"Did I?"

"*Jah.*"

Although her sister's words seemed odd, she thought back to the first outing with Bruno. He had blocked Nathanial from his offer of lunch and perhaps that extra male attention from Nathanial had spurred Bruno on to keep seeing her. That showed her that maybe Lily was right about how men thought.

"So, if you're right, what do you think I should do now?" Daisy had no one else to ask and Lily seemed so confident in what she said.

"Don't act so keen on him. He won't want you as bad if he knows he can have you."

Daisy nodded. She wanted Bruno as her husband so badly she was willing to do what her sister suggested. If it didn't work, she could always go back to the way things were. *"Denke,* Lily. I'll think about it."

"Okay. *Gut nacht."* Lily bounced out of her room without waiting for her to say good night back.

Daisy slipped further underneath her bedcovers, hoping her new plan was the right way to go.

CHAPTER 16

*A*fter breakfast, Hezekiah left for work at his brother's farm and Nancy sat at the table having a second cup of coffee. Lily was the first of the twins to come down for breakfast.

"Good morning, *Mamm.*"

"Morning, Lily. It seems Daisy has taken to sleeping in."

Lily giggled. "Probably dreaming about Bruno."

Nancy smiled. "I think you could be right."

Lily poured herself a cup of coffee and sat down at the table with her mother.

After Lily had taken a sip, Nancy said to her, "And what about you? Have you found a boy that you like?"

"*Nee,* I haven't."

Nancy hesitated a moment. "*Nee?*"

Lily's brown eyes flickered as she stared at her mother. "*Nee.*"

Against Hezekiah's better judgment, she asked her straight out, "What about Nathanial Schumacher?" She wished she could be calm and patient like her husband had suggested but she couldn't.

"He'd be the last person I would want as my boyfriend, especially after what he did to Daisy."

"That's funny, because someone said they saw you in town with him the other day."

Lily smiled, and then said, "That was the other day when I was out by myself getting things from the store. I ran into him; he talked to me, and I had to say something to be polite."

"And was that all it was?

"*Jah*, that's all it was. Why do you ask?"

Nancy shook her head. She knew Lily was lying, but if she pushed her or told her what she knew, that they'd been seen holding hands, she could very well drive her daughter away and into Nathanial's arms just like Hezekiah had warned.

"It's nothing. You know how people like to talk." She reached out and patted her daughter gently on the hand. "Forget I said anything."

"Okay."

Lily drank her coffee and then fixed herself some breakfast. All the while, Nancy sat in the kitchen restraining herself from berating her daughter for having anything to do with Nathanial Schumacher. He was trouble, just like his brother, Jacob, had been trouble.

The awful thing was that the twins were very attractive, probably the most attractive girls in the community, and they were prey for men like Nathanial. She was pleased that Daisy had found a lovely man like Bruno. If only Bruno lived locally. As much as she wanted Daisy to stay close by, if it was in God's plan that she go to Ohio, she'd have to accept it.

Daisy walked into the kitchen rubbing her eyes. "That was exciting news last night, *Mamm.* You're about to have your fourth *grosskin.*"

"I couldn't be more happy."

Daisy sat down next to her mother. "You don't look very happy."

"I am. I'm just tired."

"Do you want me to make you some breakfast, Daisy?" Lily asked.

"*Jah,* please."

"One of you will have to go out and get the eggs."

Lily said, "I'll go out and get them after breakfast. We've got enough here to make Daisy something."

Nancy nodded.

"Can I have scrambled eggs, Lily?"

"Okay."

"And when do you see Bruno next?" Nancy asked.

"Friday. He's coming here to collect me at ten in the morning. Is that okay?"

Nancy nodded. "I like Bruno and he comes from a good family." She glanced over at Lily who was whisking the eggs and Lily didn't look at her. She felt like saying that she wasn't too happy about Nathanial and his family, but she bit the inside of her lip to stop herself from blurting out words that she might later regret.

"I'm so glad you and *Dat* like him. I think he's the man I'm going to marry. I'm certain of it."

"Well, don't rush into anything. You must be certain."

"I won't rush into anything, *Mamm,* don't worry."

"I'm not worried; I trust *Gott,* so I don't worry about you girls. I know both of you will make the right decisions in finding husbands. Because you know that the decisions you make now will affect the rest of your life. Your decision must be made with your head as well as your heart; you might love someone with your heart, but if you have doubts in your head, you should listen to them."

Lily set the eggs on the stove. "That's good advice, *Mamm.* I'll remember that when I find a man I like."

"Jah, that's good advice, and both my head and my heart think that Bruno is the right man for me."

"Wait a while, Daisy. Men can put on a good act for a while, but they can't keep up that act over time. Sooner or later their true personality will shine through," *Mamm* said.

"How did you know that *Dat* was the right one for you?" Daisy asked.

"I didn't have any doubt about it whatsoever, and we knew each other for a long time, which helped as well."

"When I was in my bedroom, I thought I heard Nathanial's name mentioned," Daisy said, looking between her sister and her mother.

"Your *schweschder* ran into him at the store the other day. Someone saw her with him and told me about it. The person thought that Lily and he might have something going on."

Daisy stared at Lily. "Is that true, Lily?"

"Jah, I didn't think to mention it. I said hello, he said hello, and that's about all."

"Why didn't you tell me? We tell each other everything."

"You've been so busy with Bruno, and that's all you ever want to talk about. I didn't want to make you upset by talking about Nathanial."

Daisy nodded. "I still want you to tell me everything that's happening with you."

"And I'll tell you anything important, but bumping into him wasn't important. Don't make a fuss."

"Okay. I didn't mean to make a fuss. Stop me if I talk about Bruno too much."

Lily giggled. "It's okay. I like hearing all about him. Since I don't have romance in my life, I like to hear about it from you."

Listening to her two daughters, Nancy wouldn't have thought that anything was wrong if she hadn't known better. She knew now that Lily was very good at lying and it disturbed Nancy to learn that. There was a chance that Hezekiah's source might have been mistaken, but Hezekiah wouldn't have told her about it unless he'd been quite certain. It had to be true, and many things about the scenario scared Nancy.

CHAPTER 17

Going against Lily's advice, Daisy asked Bruno to the volleyball game on Saturday afternoon.

When they were sitting together watching the three games that were playing, Daisy asked Bruno, "Are you going to have a game?"

"I think I'll just watch unless they need an extra person to play. I'd rather sit next to you."

When he smiled at her, her insides tingled with joy.

"In that case, I'll just watch too."

He leaned close to her and said, "If we weren't surrounded by so many people right now, I'd hold your hand."

She glanced at him and gave a little giggle. Then beyond Bruno, Daisy noticed that her sister, Lily, was sitting next to Nathanial, and another girl was sitting on the other side of him. They were laughing and joking as if Nathanial was a normal person, but he wasn't a normal person—he had treated her dreadfully.

"What's wrong?" Bruno asked.

"I'm just surprised to see Lily speaking with Nathanial."

"I know you said you went on a buggy ride with him, but is he an old boyfriend of yours or something? You seem to be disturbed by him in some way."

"I know some things about him, that's all—and those things aren't good. I told you a little bit about it the other day."

Bruno turned to look over at Lily. When he turned back, he said, "What shall I do? Do you want me to do anything? Shall we tell her we need to talk to her about something, or shall I tell her you want to see her?"

Daisy was pleased that he was only too willing to help even though he didn't know the full circumstances of the matter. He was once again showing that he was a man who would stand by her no matter what.

She shook her head. "I'm probably worried about nothing. I mean, they're not alone or anything. Marcy is talking to him as well, so it should be all right."

"Let's not let him ruin our night."

"Okay, I won't."

The rest of the night, Daisy did her best to enjoy Bruno's company, but she kept an eye on Lily. Wherever Lily was, Nathanial was not far away.

WHEN THE VOLLEYBALL was drawing to a close, Daisy asked Bruno, "Do you mind if we drive Lily home with us? I'm worried she'll have Nathanial drive her home, and that won't end well."

"Of course. I don't mind at all. We must keep her out of trouble."

"*Denke.* I'll just go tell her she can come home with us."

"Okay."

She walked over to Lily and managed to get her far enough away from Nathanial to speak to her in private. "You're coming home with us soon, Lily."

"*Nee,* I don't want to do that. You should go home with him—just the two of you."

"You'll be helping me, Lily."

"How will it be helping you?"

"Remember that you said if you like someone not to act too desperate toward him?"

"*Jah?*"

"Don't you see? I have just asked Bruno to take you home as well, and he'll wonder why I don't want to be alone with him. I'm trying to keep him on his toes."

"Good work, Daisy. I'm proud of you." She glanced over at Nathanial. "It doesn't hurt to have them think you're not interested in them."

"You'll come home with us then?"

"Of course I will. Just give me a few moments. Give me ten minutes."

"I'll meet you at Bruno's buggy."

Daisy hurried back to Bruno and glanced back at Lily to see her talking with Nathanial, and he didn't look at all happy. Daisy guessed that Nathanial had planned to take her home and Lily had just given him the news that he wasn't driving her home.

Daisy was pleased that she ruined things for Nathanial. She'd have to make her sister see sense and do so without being obvious.

As soon as they got home, Lily jumped out of the buggy, thanked Bruno, and ran inside. This left Bruno and Daisy some time to say goodnight to one another.

"Daisy, would you be pleased if I stayed on for a few more months? I don't want to leave Valerie here alone and I've been offered six months' work at the horse auctions."

"Oh, Bruno. That would be *wunderbaar*," she said without realizing she'd touched him lightly on his hand.

He took hold of her hand, brought it up to his mouth, and pressed his lips gently onto her hand. She felt as though all her dreams had come true. Bruno was in love with her; she could see it in his eyes, now that he was staring at her.

"You should go inside right now, or I'll kiss you right on your beautiful lips."

She giggled. "I'm going."

He squeezed her hand a little before he released it.

"Bye," she said before she got out of his buggy.

"I'll see you soon, Daisy."

She walked inside and closed the door behind her. Her heart was thumping so hard that she could scarcely breathe. The man was in love with her. She was glad she hadn't followed Lily's advice about pretending not to be interested in him.

Looking around, she saw that her mother and father had already gone to bed. She hurried upstairs to tell Lily the good news that Bruno was staying for longer.

When she got to Lily's room, she saw that she wasn't there. She went back into her own room to see if Lily was waiting to talk with her, but she wasn't there either. Daisy checked the dark kitchen and then the bathroom, but she wasn't anywhere in the house.

The only answer was that Lily had sneaked out of the house. *She must've gone to meet Nathanial. That's why she didn't protest too hard about coming home with me and Bruno. She must've pre-arranged to meet Nathanial somewhere.*

Fuming, Daisy paced up and down, wondering what to do. She could tell her parents, but her father had a weak heart. The only thing she could do was wait until Lily came home and then she'd confront her.

Daisy being so close to Bruno had driven a wedge between herself and Lily. They'd always shared everything and Lily had never kept anything from her before.

Her thrill about Bruno was now marred by her sister's disappearance. She went back into her sister's room and looked out the window. It was then that she noticed it was slightly open and once she looked out, she saw a tree close to the house that Lily must've climbed down. And that was probably the way she'd return.

Daisy slept in Lily's bed, knowing that once Lily came back through the window, she'd find out what was going on. She'd confront her.

Lily had to take the chance that Daisy would be so tired tonight she wouldn't notice they wouldn't be having their nightly talk. She felt bad for deceiving Daisy and her parents, but she knew they didn't like Nathanial, so she felt like she was trapped. In the end, she was an adult and old enough to make her own decisions. She'd had several long talks with Nathanial and she knew they had the wrong idea about him altogether.

She opened the window, grabbed the tree branch, and swung her body onto the trunk of the tree. Stepping down each branch, she got close enough to the bottom that she could let go of the branch. Losing her balance, she landed flat on her bottom. Immediately, she sprang to her feet and hoped her dress wasn't too dirty because her mother would see it and wonder how it got stained. With her hands, she dusted down her dress and straightened it.

Peeking around the corner of the house, she saw that Bruno was driving away and Daisy was walking back to the house. As soon as Lily saw that Daisy had gone inside, she scampered to the barn in the darkness. From the barn, she stuck to the fence line and hurried down the driveway. Nathanial said he'd wait for her at the crossroads not too far from her house. Thankfully, Valerie's house was in the opposite direction so Bruno would not see him waiting there.

By the time she reached Nathanial's buggy, she was breathless.

He laughed. "What took you so long?"

"I had to wait until Bruno left the house. Daisy and Bruno were sitting in the buggy talking for the longest time. Anyway, you're lucky I'm here at all since my family doesn't approve of you." She climbed up next to him.

"I guess you're right about that." He clicked the horse onward.

"Where are we going?"

"I thought we'd go somewhere for a bite to eat." He glanced over at her. "What do you think?"

She shook her head. "Not a good idea. Someone told my *vadder* that they saw us together and close together."

"Well, a bite to eat is out of the question, then, if we are to remain a secret."

"We could just drive around for awhile. Are you hungry?"

"No hungrier than I usually am. I'll live. Is this the first time you've had to sneak out of the house?"

"Jah. It's not something I plan to make a habit of."

"How will we see each other, then, if you don't keep sneaking out? It's going to take a long time for them to forget the lies your *schweschder* told about me."

"I haven't thought about it too much."

"Fair enough."

Lily giggled. It felt good to be out, away from her parents' control, and to be able to make some decisions for herself.

He glanced over at her again. "What's funny?"

"I feel free. Free to be me."

"Shouldn't you feel like that all the time?"

"I'd like to," Lily said. "But I don't see how that's going to happen as long as I'm living under my parents' roof."

"Get a job and move out."

"I couldn't get a job. I don't know how to do anything."

"Start by doing anything you can find, any job you can get, and then you work your way up."

Lily had always thought the only way out of home was to marry and get away that way. It had never occurred to her to get a job and have her own place. "If I got a job, would that give me enough money to rent a *haus?*"

"Well, if you have no skills you probably won't get much pay at first. Not in your first job. But you could share a place with someone. That's the best way to start."

"Like who?"

He chuckled. "Look on the Internet or on notice boards. People are looking for housemates all the time."

"That sounds like a good idea. Maybe I will get a job."

"It puzzles me why you haven't had one before now."

"*Mamm* keeps Daisy and me busy, that's why. Our days are full of things to do around the *haus* and then she's got us visiting people now."

"She's teaching you to be just like her. Is that what you want, Lily?" he asked.

"*Jah,* she's got a good life and I'd like to be just like her, just not as short-tempered and cranky."

At that moment, gentle rain began to fall.

"It's raining," Nathanial said. "I just hope it doesn't get any heavier."

"I love the rain. Let's stop the buggy and walk."

"No way in the world! Then I'd be responsible if you caught a cold, or pneumonia. I'd never forgive myself."

"You could visit me and bring me hot chicken soup."

He laughed as the rain started falling more heavily. "There's no way your parents would allow me to even see you, let alone bring you anything."

"I guess that's true. I can't believe that Daisy made the whole thing up. She obviously didn't think how it would affect you."

"She was trying to get back at me. That's what I reckon."

She stared into his face as he watched the road ahead of him. "Back at you for what?"

He turned to face her. "To tell you the truth, it was so long ago that I've forgotten."

Lily giggled.

"I'm going to pull off on the side of the road somewhere. I can't watch the road and see your pretty face at the same time."

"Just let the horse go where he wants."

"Yeah, and we'll end up in a ditch. And don't forget when it's raining branches have a habit of falling off trees."

"You can't have a very good horse then, if he'll pull the buggy into a ditch."

"There's nothing wrong with Jasper. I just bought him from one of my cousins."

Lily screwed up her nose. "He looks a bit old. Is he just about to be retired?"

"*Nee.* Wait until you see him in the day; he's a real beauty." He stopped the horse at the side of the road. Then he took her hand. "I'd like to kiss you, but I don't want you to run away screaming like your *schweschder* did."

Lily laughed. "I'm not my *schweschder.*"

"Are you sure?"

Lily nodded. "Quite sure."

"How do I know you're not Daisy out to get me into more trouble?"

"Because Daisy wouldn't sneak out at night, that's how you can know."

"Ah, so you're the bad twin—the evil twin." He chuckled.

"I wouldn't say that. I just want different things out of life and I'm just beginning to find that out. I want excitement. I want to do things other people don't normally do."

"Like run in the rain?"

"*Jah*, I'd like to run in the rain without a care in the world. And if I get sick, I will worry about that when and if it happens."

"I like the sound of that. You want to live for today and tomorrow can take care of itself."

Lily laughed, and then Nathanial joined in with her laughter.

"If I lived on my own I would run in the rain right now."

"What's stopping you?" he asked. "Apart from me not wanting you to get sick?"

"Oh, that's sweet."

"Not really. I just don't want you to get sick because then I would most likely catch your cold and then I'd be sick too. Seriously though, why can't you run in the rain because you're still living at home?"

Lily sighed. "My *mudder* is like a detective. She'd somehow find my wet clothes and she'd question me. I'm not a good liar and the whole thing wouldn't end well."

He squeezed her hands just slightly. "You should seriously consider making a life for yourself. You've never gone on a *rumspringa*, have you?"

"*Nee.*"

"It figures," he said.

"Have you?"

"Yeah, not long back."

"Oh."

"We live a sheltered life. Not that I'm complaining, but I'm glad I know what else is out there."

"I don't want to know what else is out there. Why would I have to know if I'm only going to come back to the community anyway? It seems like a waste of time to me."

"I do hope you get a job, Lily. I think it would help you to get out and meet some different people. I think you'd love it."

She looked into his eyes and all that she saw was kindness. If she had believed Daisy, she wouldn't have gotten a chance to know him at all. "I'll definitely give it some serious thought. Next time I'm in town, I'll have a look at some noticeboards and see what jobs are on offer."

"Gut." He looked into the dark night as the rain was falling more steadily. "Right now I'd feel better to get you home, Lily."

"Okay."

He turned the buggy around and headed back toward her house. "What's the deal with Bruno?"

"How do you mean?"

"He seems pretty interested in Daisy and haven't they only just met?"

"You think he likes her?" Lily asked.

"Jah. I told you I bumped into them, didn't I?"

"Jah, you did—at the candy store. She was showing him around."

"I reckon they'll marry."

"Maybe." Lily felt sick to the stomach at the thought of

losing her twin and being left in the house alone with her parents. Their sole focus and attention would be on her. Besides that, she'd be lonely without her twin.

"This is about as close as I can go without everyone in your *haus* hearing the horse." He reached over the back and then handed her a thick coat. "Put this on."

"Won't you need it?"

"*Nee.* Put it over your head to keep dry."

She handed it back to him. "That's okay, it's not far."

He thrust it back into her hands. "Take it!"

"Okay." She gave a little laugh.

"I'll see you soon. Be safe."

"I will." She jumped down from the buggy, pulled the coat over her head, and hurried to the *haus.* The rain had eased and by the time she got to the bottom of the tree underneath her bedroom window, the rain had stopped.

Getting up that tree wasn't as easy as getting down. She left the coat at the bottom of the tree, intending to get it in the morning, tucked her dress into her knickers, and climbed up the tree.

Finally she reached the window. She clutched at it with both hands and then when she was deciding how to bring her legs in, a figure appeared before her. Her eyes met Daisy's.

CHAPTER 18

*D*aisy had woken suddenly when she heard a scratching sound. She'd sat up, remembering that she was in Lily's bed, waiting for her to come home and explain herself. She'd guessed the scratching noises were from Lily climbing up the tree to get back into her bedroom. Daisy squinted at the clock in the darkness to see that it was three o'clock in the morning.

She walked to the window and opened it fully. Lily clutched the window and their eyes met. Daisy pushed the window up higher and Lily made her way into the room.

"What the devil are you doing?" Daisy hissed.

With a flushed face, Lily asked, "Why are you in my room?"

"You went to meet Nathanial, didn't you?"

"Keep your voice down, or *Mamm* and *Dat* will hear you."

"What were you doing sneaking out to meet him?"

"He wanted to drive me home and he couldn't, so

133

that's why I met with him. I was trying to help you out so you wouldn't appear too keen with Bruno."

"Well, isn't that making you seem too keen on Nathanial, since you were sneaking out to meet him in the middle of the night?"

"You've all made up your mind that you don't like him and you don't even know him."

"Why would I like him? I told you what he did to me."

"He told me all about it and I know you were exaggerating. You do that sometimes. He didn't stand up for himself back then, and now he regrets it. He said it's too late to do anything about it now. I think you were unfair to him."

"Lily, what sort of man would have you meet him late at night like this? Did you stop to think about that?"

"He loves me and that's why we wanted to meet with each other. What difference is it if it's the middle of the day, or if we meet at night?"

"In the middle of the day, there are people around, but at night, he can take you somewhere deserted."

"And what—murder me? Don't be so dramatic. You're just jealous because Nathanial didn't want you and that's why you made up that story about him."

Daisy said, "Are you accusing me of lying?"

"Shush! They'll hear you."

"I don't care if they do," Daisy hollered.

"I never thought you'd be so mean to me, Daisy. You think you're better than me now because you have a boyfriend—one that *Mamm* and *Dat* like."

"I never thought you'd be so stupid."

"Get out of my room," Lily yelled.

Their mother swung the door open. "What's going on? Why aren't you girls asleep?" She looked Lily up-and-down. "Get changed and get into bed, Lily, and Daisy, you go to your own room. We'll talk about this in the morning, and no more noise. Your *vadder* has to get up early in the morning."

Daisy rushed past her mother, went into her own room, and closed the door. She jumped into bed feeling sad and alone. She'd never had a fight with her sister; this had been their first one. Why couldn't her sister see that Nathanial was no good? And how could Lily accuse her of lying about what had happened with Nathanial? She'd only been trying to protect her twin.

NANCY WENT BACK to her own room and got back into bed.

"What was all that about?" Hezekiah asked her.

"Just a squabble. I'll get to the bottom of it in the morning." She leaned over and kissed her husband on his cheek. "Go back to sleep."

A minute later, Hezekiah was snoring. Nancy was worried to see her two girls fight. There was something seriously wrong. Seeing them annoyed with each other reminded her of the ongoing fight she was having with her own sister, Nerida. Maybe it was God's way of telling her she needed to pay Nerida a visit. It wasn't right that sisters didn't get along. She made up her mind to visit Nerida the very next day, and she'd try to make amends if Nerida was willing.

CHAPTER 19

*N*ancy left the twins at home the next day. They still weren't speaking to one another, which was probably better than them yelling at one another. She'd given them jobs to do at the opposite ends of the house and hopefully that way it would break down any tension between the two of them. If they had a break from each other, they might calm down.

Nancy had no idea what their argument had been about, but guessed that Lily was a little upset that Daisy had Bruno and she had no one. Things couldn't have been easy for Lily because over the last few years they had grown used to the idea that they would marry twin brothers and they'd be together forever. Now that Daisy liked a man, it was tearing the girls apart. Nancy didn't like to see them at odds with one another, but neither could she offer a solution. It was bound to happen that one of the twins would find a man before the other. She'd had no idea that it would cause this big a problem between them.

Trying to relax, Nancy breathed in the fresh morning air. It had been raining the night before and the sweet scent of rain still filled the air. The colors of the landscape she passed looked so much brighter after a heavy downpour. The greens of the pastures were so much more vibrant, the roads darker, and her neighbors' red barns were now standing out in stark contrast to the trees behind them.

Her horse's hoofs swished through the puddles and Nancy skillfully navigated around some potholes made a little worse by the recent weather. As she got closer to Nerida's, she hoped the right words would come into her head when she was in front of her sister.

She stopped the buggy close to Nerida's house and when she'd tied the horse to the fencepost, she walked right up to the front door and knocked on it quickly before she could change her mind.

The door opened and Willow, her young niece, answered the door. "It's nice to see you, Aunt Nancy. Come in."

"Are you sure it's okay?"

"*Jah, Mamm* saw you coming from the kitchen window. She's waiting in the kitchen for you."

"Okay. Where's Violet?"

"She's upstairs writing a letter. I'll go and tell her you're here, but I think *Mamm* wants to talk to you by herself first." Willow wrapped her arms around Nancy. "I'm glad you're here."

"Me too, Willow. It's been too long."

Nancy closed the front door behind her and headed into the kitchen.

Nerida was sitting at the table with her hands firmly clasped in front of her. "Hello, Nancy. What brings you here today?"

Nancy walked forward. "I've come to say I'm sorry. It's silly that we have such a rift that's been developing between us because of ... I barely remember how it started." Nancy knew very well how it started, but didn't want to dredge it all up again.

"You can sit down." Nerida motioned with her hand toward the chair opposite.

Nancy pulled out the chair and sat down.

Her younger sister continued, "I was very hurt by what happened."

Nancy nodded. "I was irritated by you and I won't say that I wasn't, but I shouldn't have let that come between the two of us. It doesn't really matter that you gave your girls similar names to my girls'."

Nerida shook her head. "Are we going to start this whole thing over again? My *dochders'* names are nothing like your girls' names."

"But don't you see that they are? My girls have flower names and then you called your daughters Violet and Willow."

Nerida rolled her eyes and sighed. "I don't have to explain myself, but I will. I'd always liked the name 'Violet,' and while I realize it is a flower, it's also a color. I have always liked the name 'Willow,' which is a tree and not a flower. When I named them, I didn't name them purposely to copy your flower idea."

"I told you how I felt when you were considering calling your *boppli* Violet. And yet, you went ahead with the name. You were always copying me when we were children and I thought you'd stop when we became adults."

"I didn't think you would be that upset about it. Anyway, I copied you when we were younger because I looked up to you. You're my only *schweschder*. I wasn't going to copy my brothers, was I?" Nerida raised her eyebrows and her mouth lifted upward into a kind smile.

Nancy gave a little laugh. "I suppose not."

"Was I that annoying?"

Tears came to Nancy's eyes as she remembered the good times they'd had growing up together. "You weren't annoying at all; we had fun. It was only when you got older that you became annoying."

"I didn't copy you or imitate you deliberately. I guess I thought the things that you did were good ideas. I can't even remember how I copied you back then, but I must've because I can remember you complaining about it when we were teenagers."

"It doesn't matter any more." Nancy wiped a tear from her eye. "I was silly to get annoyed with you and let this huge rift develop."

Nerida smiled. *"Jah,* you were. We should've been close and our *kinner* would now be closer than they are."

In her heart, Nancy still believed that her sister had copied her idea and nothing Nerida could say or do would persuade her into believing otherwise. All the same, as much as she was irritated by what her sister had done, they were sisters and she was prepared to put the past aside to have Nerida and Nerida's husband, John, and their two girls, Violet and Willow, back in her life and the life of her family.

CHAPTER 20

*W*hile their mother was out trying to make things right with Nerida, Daisy didn't want a similar rift to develop between herself and Lily.

She walked over to Lily, who'd been given the job of washing the windows outside the house.

"What do you want?" Lily asked when she saw Daisy approaching.

"You don't have to speak like that."

"Well, I think I do. You've shown that you don't care about me now that you're seeing a lot of Bruno."

"Is that what this is about?"

Lily threw the wet sponge on the ground. "You tell me."

"You know what Nathanial is like."

"I don't, and I can do anything I want. No one cares about me anyway."

"You're only saying that to be dramatic, or do you think *Mamm* and *Dat* don't care about you now?"

"You'll get married soon and then everyone will be

married except me. It didn't turn out like we always said it would. We were supposed to be married at the same time."

"And if I could've kept my word, I would've, but Bruno doesn't have a twin."

"Did you ever stop and think that he might not be the right person for you? We haven't traveled to all the different communities yet like we said we would. If we do that, we could find twins."

"Nee!" Daisy shook her head. "I can't, now that I have met Bruno."

"Bruno, Bruno, Bruno—that's all I ever hear about anymore. That's all you ever speak about all the time. I'm sick of it!" She picked up the metal bucket full of water and threw it down on the ground.

Once the water drained, Lily picked up the bucket and hurled it at the window in anger. The window shattered and glass went everywhere.

Daisy looked on in horror as the scene unfolded.

"I'll go away and then you'll be happy." Lily pulled a sour face at Daisy before stomping down the driveway with her hands curled into fists.

Daisy carefully picked up the larger pieces of glass and laid them down together so she could cover them in newspaper later. Instead of running after Lily, she figured she would give her time to cool down. It was clear that nothing she could say at this point would make any difference. Once she was back in the house, Daisy found some brown paper that they used for making dress patterns and then she found some tape. She taped up the glass in the paper and then threw it in the trash.

Once she'd cleaned up as best she could, she looked around the yard and down along the driveway, but she couldn't see Lily anywhere.

Lily was down the driveway and just about to turn onto the road when she remembered Nathanial's coat at the bottom of her bedroom window. How would she explain that if anyone found it? That was a disaster waiting to happen. She turned around and headed back to the house hoping Daisy wouldn't see her. It was unfortunate that the window broke because she hadn't thrown the bucket very hard. It must've been a weak or faulty window. Maybe the bucket hit the window in the wrong place.

When she got back to the house, she couldn't see Daisy anywhere. Directly under her bedroom window at the back of the house, she found Nathanial's coat, from the night before, just where she'd left it underneath the tree. After she had looked around about her to make sure no one was watching, she grabbed it and curled it into a tight ball. She headed into the barn where she'd hide the coat until she went somewhere to meet Nathanial again.

She tucked the coat behind the drum of chicken feed, and then sat down on a bail of hay and cried. It felt like Daisy had left her already and the only person who understood her was Nathanial and her parents didn't approve of him. How was her life ever going to get any better? It seemed as though Daisy would definitely marry Bruno, and what would become of her? Nathanial was right. She'd have to get a job and make a life on her own. It was a hard thing to do since she'd always had her twin with her every day of her life. Lily stretched her hands above her head and yawned. It had been a tough couple of days. She arranged some hay bales together, lay down on them, and slowly closed her eyes.

Then, she sat up quickly. All she wanted to do was see Nathanial, the only person who understood her. He'd understand why she broke that window. She grabbed his coat, spread it out, and then she wrapped it around her to keep herself warm. Being in his warm coat comforted her.

NANCY'S BUGGY horse clipped-clopped steadily up the driveway. Nancy immediately noticed the brown paper covering the window at the front of the house. Before she unhitched the buggy, she rushed into the house to see what was going on.

"What on earth happened to the window?" she asked Daisy when she found her in the kitchen.

Daisy swung around looking incredibly guilty.

"Lily and I had an argument and then there was an accident with the window and it's broken."

"I can see that it's broken, but how could that possibly have come about?"

Daisy shrugged her shoulders and her perfectly shaped mouth kept tightly closed. Nancy had never been able to figure out which twin did what. They'd always covered for one another and clearly that wasn't about to change even though they were at odds with one another.

"Where's Lily now?" Nancy demanded.

"She was upset and went for a walk. I'm sure she'll be back soon."

Nancy sighed. "We'll have to get someone out to fix

the window. Your *vadder* won't be too happy about it when he gets home."

"Sorry, *Mamm*."

Nancy gritted her teeth. "Sorry won't fix the window!"

"*Jah*, you're right." Then Daisy smiled brightly. "How did things go with Aunt Nerida?"

"Make me a cup of tea while I unhitch the buggy, then I'll tell you all about it."

"Is it good news, then?"

"*Jah*. Well, it's not bad news."

HOURS LATER, it was growing dark and Lily still hadn't come home. Daisy got more worried. What if she'd driven Lily into Nathanial's arms?

Daisy was helping her mother with dinner. "Where could Lily be? It's past time for her to get home. It's nearly time for *Dat* to get home."

"You know her better than anybody. Where do you think she'd be?" her mother asked.

Daisy bit her lip. "I'll take the buggy out and look for her."

"Okay, but don't go by yourself. Stop by Valerie's house and see if Bruno will go with you."

"Great; okay."

CHAPTER 21

*N*ancy took Daisy by the arm. "Come on. I'll help you hitch the buggy. Try to find her before your *vadder* gets home because I don't want him to get worried."

"I will."

Together they got the buggy ready before it got dark. They used the fastest horse, not the one her mother had just taken out that day to visit Nerida. A fresher horse could travel better.

Daisy was upset. She should've let things cool off more before she spoke to Lily. Valerie's house was on the way to the Schumachers' house.

When Daisy arrived at Valerie's, she jumped down from the buggy, hurried over, and knocked on the door. She had hoped that Bruno would answer the door, but it was Valerie.

Seeing the look on Daisy's face, Valerie asked, "What's wrong?"

"I was wondering if I might be able to borrow Bruno for a short time?"

"Is something wrong?" Valerie asked again.

By this time, Bruno was at the door standing next to his sister.

"Daisy, what's going on?"

"It's Lily. She's disappeared and hasn't come home. We had a dreadful argument. I'm trying to find her before my *vadder* gets home. He tends to worry and he's got a problem with his heart."

"Okay. I'll come with you. Don't worry; we'll find her." He looked back at his sister. "You go ahead and eat dinner; don't worry about me. I'll grab something later."

Valerie walked out the door and stood on the porch as they were both getting into the buggy. "Is there anything I can do, Daisy?"

"Please pray that she'll be safe."

"I will."

Bruno had immediately taken control and sat in the driver's seat.

As they headed down to the main road, he asked, "Where are we going?"

"The Schumachers' *haus.* Nathanial is staying at Matthew Schumacher's—they're cousins."

"Is this the same Nathanial I met the other day?"

"Jah. She's developed a friendship with him but I think she's only doing it to upset me."

Bruno glanced at her and she shook her head.

"Don't ask. It's a long story."

"I didn't ask anything. Can you think of anywhere else she might be?"

"If she's not there, we could just check with all our friends. I don't know where else she would be."

"Don't worry, we'll find her."

"Denke for coming with me."

"I'm glad you asked me."

WHEN THEY PULLED up at the Schumachers' house, Daisy said, "You stay here. I'll run in and see if she's inside, or if she's been here."

"Okay."

Daisy knocked on the door, trying not to look worried.

Matthew opened the door and, knowing which twin stood before him, said, "Hello, Daisy."

"Hi, Matthew. Lily wouldn't happen to be here, would she?"

"Nee. Why?"

"She's missing."

Matthew yelled over his shoulder, "Nathanial, have you seen Lily Yoder?"

"Not today I haven't."

Relief washed over Daisy. If Nathanial was here, it meant that Lily wasn't with him. Then again, if Lily wasn't with him, where could she possibly be?

"She's missing!" Matthew yelled again to Nathanial, who came to the door as quick as a flash.

"Is that right, Daisy? Is Lily missing?"

"I'm sure it's nothing to worry about. She's probably just at someone's *haus* visiting and she forgot to tell us."

"Then why do you look so worried?" Nathanial asked.

"Because she is my *schweschder*," Daisy said a little too harshly.

Matthew suggested, "Why don't we join you, and that way we can cover more ground?"

Daisy agreed, glad that Matthew knew all of Daisy and Lily's friends. They decided that Daisy and Bruno would call at all the houses south of the Schumacher property, and Mark and Nathanial would do the ones to the north. Then they'd meet back at the Yoders' house when they were finished. By now, Daisy's father would be home and would know about Lily's disappearance.

When Daisy got back into the buggy, she explained the plan to Bruno.

As the buggy traveled back down the road, Bruno asked, "Is that a good thing that she wasn't with Nathanial?"

"I am relieved in a way, but I'm worried because I still don't know where she is."

"I'm sure there's nothing to worry about; she's probably just visiting a friend or something."

Daisy shook her head. "We had a dreadful fight and a window even got broken. We never ever had an argument before—it was terrible."

TWO HOURS LATER, they got back to the house without Lily. Nancy rushed out to the buggy.

"We've just found her. She came back here just five minutes ago."

"That's a relief," Bruno said.

"Where was she?" Daisy asked, now finding herself annoyed at Lily for wasting all their time.

"I don't know. She hasn't said yet. She's inside talking to your *vadder*."

"I'll take Bruno home and come back."

Bruno said, "Why don't I bring the buggy back in the morning? I can put the horse in Valerie's stable overnight. You stay here now; you're tired."

Her mother stepped forward. *"Denke*, Bruno. I think it would be a good idea."

"You don't have to thank me." He gave Daisy's mother a big smile, and then said to Daisy, "I'll see you in the morning, early."

Bruno left, and before Nancy and Daisy got back inside the house, Nathanial and Matthew drove up in Matthew's buggy. Daisy had temporarily forgotten that they were out looking for Lily.

"Mamm, that's Nathanial and Matthew Schumacher. They were helping us look for Lily."

Nancy raised her eyebrows. "Ask them if they want to come in for a hot chocolate."

Nancy went back into the house and Daisy rushed over and thanked the two young men for looking for Lily.

"She's in the house; she's okay. I've just got home myself this minute, so I don't know where she's been or anything."

"She's all right, though?" Matthew asked.

Daisy nodded.

"I'm glad she's okay," Nathanial said.

"Would you like to come in for a hot drink?"

"We won't stay, Daisy. We've both got to get up early for work in the morning," Matthew said.

"*Denke* very much for looking. You saved Bruno and me hours looking for her."

CHAPTER 22

*D*aisy walked into the kitchen and saw Lily sitting down next to their father.

"Are they coming inside, Daisy?" her mother asked.

Lily looked up at Daisy anxiously. *"Nee,* I can't face anyone."

Daisy shook her head. "They said they had to get up early for work tomorrow."

"I should go to bed," Lily said.

Daisy ignored Lily's words, turned around, and walked out of the room and hurried upstairs before Lily.

Daisy got ready for bed behind her closed door. She took off her prayer *kapp,* and changed into her night-gown. She was too exhausted to brush out her hair as she normally did.

When she'd just dozed off, she felt someone rocking her shoulder. She opened her eyes to see Lily.

"I'm sorry, Daisy."

Daisy sat up in bed. "What made you so angry?"

"I just thought no one cared about me and it looks like you'll soon be married to Bruno and then what will happen to me? Of course, I want you to be happy, but I want me to be happy as well. I want us both to be happy together like always. Everything is changing."

Daisy imagined how she would feel if Lily had found a man to marry before she had met Bruno. "I understand, Lily. It's hard because we've always been so close, and things are changing. I think Bruno likes me as much as I like him and we'll probably marry, but I can't say when."

"You'll marry him and probably soon."

Daisy giggled.

"Can we be friends again?" Lily asked.

"Always. Even when we were arguing, we were closer than two people could ever be."

In the warm glow from the light flooding out of Lily's room across the hall, Daisy saw Lily's sad face break into a smile.

"You know what I found out from tonight?" Daisy asked.

"What?

"I'm pretty sure Matthew is very keen on you."

"I kind of thought that he was, but so is Nathanial."

"Matthew is much nicer," Daisy assured her.

"I know."

"I guess you have to make up your own mind about that."

"Can we talk more tomorrow?"

Daisy nodded. *"Jah,* and then you can tell me where you disappeared to tonight."

Lily gave a little giggle before she leaned over and gave her sister a tight hug. "Are things back to normal between us?" Lily asked.

"Of course they are."

When Lily walked out of her room, Daisy slipped back under the covers wondering how she would feel if Lily got married first. Although she liked Bruno, she still didn't know if Bruno liked her enough to marry her. He'd come close to marrying once before and hadn't followed through with it. Perhaps a private talk with Valerie would give her some insight.

WHEN NANCY GOT into bed with her husband, she whispered, "With all the fuss over Lily, I forgot to tell you I visited Nerida today."

"How did that go?"

"I think it went well. We're probably not back to being the best of friends, but I think we made a good start."

"Did you apologize to her?"

"For what? Do you think I was in the wrong?"

"It was so long ago that I don't remember what happened or if there was a 'right and wrong' situation. Sometimes both people can be in the wrong and in the right depending on which person is viewing the situation. Being right isn't important when it's about family, and in saying that, I'm not thinking that you were in the wrong."

Nancy listened hard to her husband as he struggled to dig himself out of the hole that he had just dug for himself. Even though she knew she'd had cause to be angry with Nerida, in hindsight, she probably should have kept her opinions to herself.

"I would certainly do things differently now. I would keep my mouth shut for one thing."

"It's often best that we hold our tongues and think before we say things."

"Do you think I should've kept quiet?" Nancy asked.

"I'm speaking about people in general. Our words can hurt deeply."

"*Jah.* I've learned that lesson the hard way."

"Tell me what you said to Nerida?"

"I just said I'm sorry that we haven't been speaking and I'd like things to go back to the way they were."

"And she accepted that?"

"It'll take time to get back to where we were, but we had a good talk. I think we'll be okay."

"I'm pleased. What made you take the step of visiting her?"

"Lily and Daisy were fighting, and then I saw how silly they were being. It upset me that two of the people I love most in the world were fighting."

"That's how our Heavenly Father must feel when his children fight among themselves."

"That's true. I didn't think about it like that. We've missed out on many years together and our *kinner* could've been closer."

"Looks like things are working out for everybody, then," Hezekiah said.

"I hope so. I hope this is the end of Daisy and Lily

quarreling. Daisy was very concerned when Lily disappeared."

"We all were."

CHAPTER 23

Daisy was awake early the next morning so she'd be able to take Bruno back to Valerie's when he brought the buggy back from the night before. Daisy's father had just left for work, and Lily still wasn't awake.

She sat across from her mother as they both ate breakfast.

"Are you and Lily getting along better? I heard you whispering and giggling last night. Did you patch up your differences?"

"I think so. I think she feels left out that I've got Bruno and she's got no one."

"I was worried that she might like Nathanial."

Daisy shook her head. "I don't think she likes Nathanial. I think she was just pleased that he was showing her some attention. I think that's all over with now."

"She's come to her senses about him?"

"I think so. In fact, I'm sure she has."

"That must be hard for her that you've got someone

and she doesn't. You've always been so close and done everything together. I was afraid this would happen one day. I didn't think there would be a big falling out between you, but I knew one of you would be sad without the other. You both built up in your minds that you would live in the same place and marry brothers."

"And marry *twin* brothers," Daisy corrected her mother.

"It wasn't likely to ever be like that."

"I suppose not," Daisy had to agree.

"Do you know where Lily went last night?"

"I think she just went for a walk. She hasn't really said."

"Sometimes it's good to be alone to think things through. Do you know what time Bruno is getting here?" her mother asked.

"It would have to be early, before he goes to work. I suppose there was no hurry to get the buggy back."

"Well, everyone was too upset to think straight last night."

The sound of hoofbeats distracted them. Daisy ran to the window and was pleased to see that it was Bruno.

"I'll be back soon, *Mamm.* I just have to drop him back at Valerie's."

"I'll see you when I see you."

Daisy threw on her black shawl and hurried out to Bruno.

"How are you feeling this morning?" he asked when she climbed into the buggy next to him.

"I'm feeling fine. Lily and I are okay now; we sorted everything out."

"What was the problem?"

Daisy shook her head. "It's a little complicated."

He gave a quick laugh. "Things between families usually are." He turned the buggy around and headed down to the road. "Take my *mudder* for instance; she wrote me a letter saying she wanted me to come home."

"Ach nee! Are you going home soon—sooner than you said?"

He smiled at her. "I've got a letter back in Valerie's buggy that I will send to her today, and that letter tells my *mudder* that I have met someone very special and that is why I need to stay here longer."

Daisy's face lit up. "You said that to your *mudder?"*

"I put that in a letter and I just wondered if it's okay with you if I send that letter? I mentioned you by name, if you don't mind."

Daisy's heart flooded with gladness. This man was telling his mother about her by name. "I don't mind at all."

"Valerie's got a phone in the barn and my *mudder* could've called, but she prefers to write. I'm going to the post office when I get a chance today and I'll post that letter."

"How's Valerie?"

"If you don't need to go home right away, how about you stop by and talk to her?"

"I was thinking of doing that. Is she awake?"

"Jah. She is. I'm running a little late for work, but I've already got my buggy hitched and ready to take me to work." He gave a little laugh. "When I say 'my' buggy, I mean Valerie's buggy. She's been good enough to allow me to use it while I'm here."

"I'll stay on and speak with her before I go home."

"Daisy, I won't be able to see you much because of how much I'll be working, but would you come and have a picnic with me on Sunday afternoon after the meeting?"

"*Jah,* I'd like that."

"I'll arrange everything. I don't want you to lift a finger."

"Okay."

When Bruno drove away, Daisy knocked on Valerie's front door.

"Coming." Valerie opened the door. "Daisy!"

"I hope you don't mind me coming to say hello. Bruno said you were awake."

"Please come in. I'm getting sick of my own company. Come and sit with me. Have you had breakfast?"

"I have."

"How about a cup of tea?"

"I can always do with a cup of hot tea."

"Good. I have just boiled the water."

Daisy sat down at the kitchen table, watching Valerie make the tea. "How have you been?"

"I guess I'm doing okay; I'm adjusting. I don't know what I'll do when Bruno goes back; he's been such a good help to me."

"It's good that he might be staying here for a few more months."

"It's a blessing." Valerie placed a cup of tea in front of her. "Do you have milk or sugar?"

"*Nee,* just black is fine for me, *denke.*"

"How is Lily doing? She disappeared or something for a while last night?"

"She's okay now. We had a bit of an argument and a

164

window got broken accidentally. It was a bit of a fuss, but we're okay now. Everyone was panicked looking for her, but she hadn't gone far at all."

"That's good." Valerie sat down alongside her.

Daisy wondered what to say to her; she was used to talking to much younger women and Valerie was closer to her mother's age. "Bruno tells me that his mother had a woman lined up for him to marry."

Valerie laughed. *"Jah.* That seems to be what mothers do."

"Did your *mudder* match you with Dirk?" Daisy nearly spilled her tea. It wasn't the wisest thing to bring up the subject of Valerie's late husband just weeks after he had been found dead, although, Valerie had spoken of him before and hadn't minded. "I'm sorry. I shouldn't have mentioned your husband. I'm so stupid sometimes. *Mamm* always says I speak before I think."

"Don't be sorry about that. I want to talk about him. I feel that he's close to me when I speak of him."

Relieved, Daisy listened while Valerie told her all about Dirk and how they had met. Valerie shed a few tears, which brought sympathy tears to Daisy's eyes.

"It wasn't all smooth sailing in our marriage. Most marriages are like that. It's not easy getting used to living with another person."

Daisy nodded and sipped on her hot tea.

"But the problem at the start of our relationship didn't help at all."

"Do you want to talk about it?" Daisy asked.

Valerie didn't wait to be asked twice and lunged into her story. "Dirk had always loved me. I didn't love him because there was someone else in my life and Dirk knew it."

"What happened and how did you come to marry Dirk? Did you realize it was he who you really loved all along?"

"*Nee.* The man I loved went to another county and married someone else quite quickly. I was devastated and it took me a long time to get over it. Dirk was there for me. I wasn't in love with him when we married, but I grew to love him. It was a different kind of love to the love I had for that first man. I can't even describe how that love was. It was something all-encompassing and I'm sure not many people experience that kind of love." Valerie's whole body trembled. "Unfortunately, it must have all been one-sided. It was all going on in my head and wasn't real. If it had been real, there's no way he could've married anyone else."

Daisy found Valerie's story quite sad. "I find it all confusing. So many people tell me different things about love. I know some married couples aren't happy, and others are. Some start off happy and then don't remain that way."

"It's a complicated thing," Valerie said, now smiling.

"I suppose it was good that that first man moved away. It would've been hard to see him all the time with another woman."

"*Jah,* you're right. It would've been dreadful, but he eventually left my mind and my heart after he betrayed me. I felt hurt at first, but nothing lasts forever—not pain, anyway."

"I'm glad." Valerie was such a kind and gentle person that Daisy didn't want to see her upset.

"Have you ever experienced love at your young age, Daisy?"

Daisy carefully set her teacup back on the saucer. "Between you and me, I like your *bruder.*"

Valerie laughed and Daisy was relieved that she was taking the news well. "I could tell that from the moment you walked in the door—that there was something between the two of you."

That was something Daisy needed to know. She didn't want to be like Valerie and think that the man she loved felt the same and then find out that he'd married somebody else. She couldn't think of anything worse.

"Jah, well, I don't know if we could call it love, but I like him, strongly."

"You seem a very good match."

"Do you think so? You don't think I'm too young for him?"

"Age has little to do with it. He's attracted to your personality and the way you light up the room when you walk into it with your cheerfulness."

Daisy giggled. "I didn't know I did that."

Valerie swiped her hand through the air. "So many people are stuffy and boring, and so serious. That gets tiresome after a while."

"It does, doesn't it?"

"If I had been blessed enough to have a daughter, I would have wanted her to be just like you."

"You would make a *wunderbaar mudder,* Valerie, and

your *dochder* would've been blessed to have you in her life."

Valerie laughed. "Denke. I've grown used to the fact that that is something that I will never have."

Daisy cleared her throat. "If you don't mind me asking, did you have something medically wrong with you that made you not able to have *kinner?*"

"No, nothing. If I did have anything wrong with me, I didn't know about it."

"Maybe Dirk had the problem."

"Maybe. We'll never know because he refused to get tested, and then we ran out of time. It just wasn't meant to be."

"Tulip's going through that right now. She desperately wants to have a baby and nothing is happening. It seems to be making her upset. I haven't talked to her about it, but I know she desperately wants to have a *boppli.*"

"She's got plenty of time before she needs to start worrying about it. It can take years sometimes. I wouldn't want to see anyone childless."

"I guess it's something that most people just take for granted," Daisy said.

"You're right, Daisy. I know I did. It was the natural progression of getting married. There was so much pressure on young people to get married back then. The next thing was to have *bopplis.*"

Daisy took another sip of her tea, wondering what her future would bring. She didn't mind too much if she didn't have any children, because she already had nieces and one nephew, and she knew she would get a whole lot more too. "Were you under pressure to marry Dirk?"

"I suppose I was under pressure to marry somebody. Everyone married so young back then, at seventeen and eighteen. I was nearly twenty and didn't want to remain unmarried. Since I was the oldest girl in the *familye*, I felt a certain amount of pressure to make a good example and there was also the financial burden I was to my parents." Valerie shook her head. "Nothing was said, but I knew that once I married and left the family home there would be one less mouth to feed."

"But also one less person to do all the chores," Daisy pointed out.

Valerie chuckled, "Very true, but there were plenty of girls in the family to do the chores."

"If you don't mind me saying, Valerie, I think it's a bit awful that you felt you had to move out of your home for financial reasons. Couldn't you have gotten a job?"

"Very few women worked back then. It's not like it is today where most women work out of the home. They were different times."

"I'm glad I didn't live back then. If I did, *Mamm* and *Dat* would've already given up on me and probably kicked me out."

"Or they would have found you someone to marry two years ago."

"*Jah, Mamm* likes to match-make, I know that for sure and for certain."

"Yet, she hasn't found anyone for you?" Valerie laughed. "She mightn't want you and Lily to leave since you're the last two—the youngest."

Daisy giggled. "I think she would love us to go. Half the time I think Lily and I drive her crazy."

"I can't see how that would be true," Valerie said.

"It is." Daisy took another sip of tea.

"I've got cookies somewhere. Would you like some?"

"Nee denke, I'm fine."

"More tea?"

"Nee, I've not finished this one yet." Daisy took the last mouthful and set the teacup down. "I should go now."

"Can't you stay longer, Daisy?"

Daisy was a little surprised that she'd want her to stay. "Okay, if you want me to. There's nowhere that I have to be in particular."

"I'd like if you could stay a little longer."

"Then I might have that second cup of tea."

Valerie stood and took hold of the teacup in front of her. "I'll find those cookies too."

When Daisy left an hour later, she was pleased she'd stopped by to visit Valerie. Once she'd gotten past the initial awkwardness, it had been just like talking with a friend her own age, and Valerie had seemed better afterward.

As she drove the buggy home, down the narrow, winding tree-lined roads, her thoughts went to Tulip and how she must feel watching Rose so happy about being pregnant. Now that Daisy wasn't getting along with Lily all that well, she realized she wasn't as close to Rose and Tulip as she would like to be. Now was a perfect time to change that.

CHAPTER 24

*D*aisy arrived back home with a plan. She called Tulip and told her they'd all collect her and then continue on to visit Rose. Tulip loved the idea.

Daisy ran into the house and found her mother and Lily in the kitchen. *"Mamm,* guess what?"

Her mother stopped sweeping and leaned on the broom. "What is it that's got you so excited?"

"You, me, and Lily are going to visit Rose. We'll collect Tulip on the way. We haven't visited her since she told us she's pregnant. I've called Tulip and she's getting ready."

"I think it's a great idea," Nancy said. "Have you called Rose?"

"Nee, not yet."

"Why don't you call Rose to see if she's got anything on today? She might be busy."

"Can't it be a surprise? Mark and she only have one buggy between them, and she's not going to walk anywhere in her condition, especially since she's had two miscarriages. She said she was going to rest until the *boppli's* born. She'll be home for certain."

"All the same, she might have visitors. Call her and see if we can stop by."

"Okay." Daisy hurried out to the barn to make the call. It was a waste of time to call Rose to see if she was going to be home and Daisy knew it, but her mother always had to do things a certain way—her way.

When Daisy came back into the house to deliver the news that Rose was home and looking forward to their visit, her mother had come up with another idea.

"You and Lily will stay home today and clean the *haus*. I will collect Tulip and go on to visit Rose on my own. What's more, as punishment, you're both not allowed to leave the *haus* for a week and you'll come straight home after the meeting on Sunday."

"But *Mamm*, Bruno has a special thing planned for us on Sunday after the meeting. He's making us a picnic. And besides that, it was my idea for us all to visit Rose."

"You can call Bruno and tell him it'll have to be postponed."

"But *Mamm*, I think he's going to propose."

"You should've thought about that before you broke the window."

Lily jumped in and said, "I broke the window. It had nothing to do with Daisy. I picked up the bucket and hurled it in a temper—a filthy rotten temper."

"It doesn't matter to me who threw it," *Mamm* said.

"Daisy shouldn't be punished the something that I did. It's not fair."

"Both of you are being punished for acting like children when you're old enough to act like young ladies." She shook her head at them. "What time did you tell Tulip we were coming?"

"At eleven," Daisy answered.

"I should hurry."

They watched at the doorway while their mother went on the visit to Rose that Daisy had planned.

"It's so unfair," Lily said.

"I know, I can't believe she'd do it. It's my idea. I just wanted us to spend more time with Rose and Tulip. Also, I don't mind staying home today, but Sunday was going to be special—I'm certain of it. Now that's all been ruined thanks to *Mamm.*"

Lily smiled. "Don't worry. Perhaps she'll change her mind before then. She wants us married, so she'll see sense before Sunday. Why don't we cook a really nice dinner and clean the *haus* well?"

Daisy sighed and then shook her head. *"Nee,* it won't make a difference. She'll expect nothing less. I think we're done for. It's no use. She's never gone back on her word when she's punished us before. We're being treated like children."

NANCY DROVE off laughing at her two daughters, who stared at her out the window with deliberate sad faces. They had no idea they were about to get a visitor. Earlier that morning, Hezekiah had arranged to have the glass replaced in the broken window by placing a phone call to the Bontragers, the local Amish glaziers.

Ed Bontrager had said he'd send his oldest son, Elijah,

out that morning. Elijah would be perfect for one of her daughters, and since Daisy only had eyes for Bruno, Nancy had a hunch that Elijah could be the man to take Lily's mind off Nathanial. The Bontragers were quiet and kept to themselves. There were five boys all close in age. Nancy figured Elijah was around the same age as Tulip—just a little older than the twins. Ed's wife had died years ago and Ed had never remarried.

Nancy pulled up the buggy at Tulip's house and waited for her to come out. It had been a while since she'd had some quiet time with just Tulip and Rose without the constant mindless chatter of the twins. Rose would want to talk about her coming baby and Nancy wanted to share that joy with her, while reassuring Tulip that her turn would come soon.

TWO HOURS LATER, the girls were up to their armpits in housework when they heard loud hoofbeats working their way to the house. They both hurried to the door, thinking it was their mother back early, and they were surprised to see the oldest Bontrager boy, Elijah, in a wagon.

He jumped down and waved and the girls walked toward him.

"Hello there. You've got a broken window?"

"*Jah,* we do," Daisy said while Lily stood still, gawking at him.

"I've come to measure it."

"You're going to fix it?" Lily asked as she stepped forward.

He smiled. "I am. I'll measure it first and then go back to the factory and cut the glass. You'll have a new windowpane by the end of the day."

"Wunderbaar!" Daisy glanced at her sister who was looking very interested in Elijah.

He was tall and fair-haired, and his build was slight rather than the solid build she knew her sister preferred, but surely his relaxed, friendly manner and good character made up for his physique.

"Lily, why don't you show Elijah the broken window? I've got that pot on the stove I've got to watch."

"Jah, right this way, Elijah."

Daisy smiled as she watched her twin sister walk to the front of the house with Elijah. She had nothing on the stove and Lily had played along without missing a beat, thanks to the like minds the twins shared.

"How did the window break?" he asked, standing there staring at it.

"It was just my clumsy sister. She was washing the floor and the end of the broom smashed into the window."

He took hold of the jagged pieces of glass left in the window and carefully placed them on the ground. Then he looked in the window. "It was broken from the outside."

Lily did her best act of looking surprised. "Was it?"

"Jah, it was."

She followed his gaze to the metal bucket just to the side in the garden.

"I'm not really sure what happened," she said, fluttering her lashes.

He gave her a smile before he took his tape out of the pocket of his work pants. She stood back a little and watched him take the measurements. He then crouched down and set the tape on the ground and jotted the measurements on a small notepad.

"That's the smallest notepad I've ever seen."

He looked up at her. "That's all I need. Just a few measurements and the width of the glass." He held it up in the air and then stood. "And it fits in my pocket."

"Do all your brothers work in the glass business?"

"Most of us, but not all of us. Here." He held the small pad and pen out to Lily. "Hold this for me, would you?"

She took it from him while he took a couple more measurements. Then he spun around and took the notepad from her.

He didn't seem interested in her at all, and was only polite. Most of the young men gave her more attention and it bothered her that he didn't.

"Denke. That's all I need for now."

"That's it?"

"Jah." He gave her a polite nod and then strode off toward his wagon.

She hurried after him. "What's the process now then—with the glass?"

"Like I said, I take the measurements back and cut the glass. I'll be back later."

"Can I come and watch?"

He stopped suddenly and turned around to face her. "It's dangerous in the factory if you don't know what you're doing."

"I could watch from a safe distance."

"My *vadder* wouldn't like it."

A cheeky grin spread across Lily's face. "Do you always do what your *vadder* wants?"

"Jah, I do." He climbed into the wagon and said over his shoulder, "It's his factory."

Lily stood there and watched him leave. Her cute flirty act had always worked in the past, particularly with Nathanial.

WHEN ELIJAH RETURNED with the glass, Lily headed out to talk with him. He had parked his wagon as close to the window as he could.

"Don't you need two men to lift that?"

"Nee, I can do it by myself, Daisy."

"It's Lily. And I just asked because it must be heavy."

"I do it all the time by myself. It's not a big window."

"Oh, you must be very strong. Can I see your muscles?" She stepped forward with an outstretched hand to touch his bicep and he moved away.

"Nope."

While he untied the ropes that secured the glass in the back of the wagon, Lily wondered how she could engage him in conversation. There were only so many questions she could ask about glass. "You don't go to many of the young people's outings."

"That's because I'm not young."

Lily laughed. "You're young enough."

"I've got other things to do."

Lily stepped closer with her hands behind her back. "Like what?"

"Working keeps me busy."

"You can't work all the time," she said.

He answered without looking up at her. "I don't, but when I'm not working I just want to sit and do nothing."

"Well, that just sounds boring. You need to enjoy yourself more." She was pleased when he finally took his eyes off what he was doing and looked at her.

"You might want to move back a few steps because I'll need to swing the glass that way."

She frowned and stepped back. "Is this far enough?"

He looked across at her. "Yep, that'll do it." After he slipped on some large gloves, he took hold of the glass and carried it to the window.

Lily was so offended at the way he was treating her, she went into the house and closed the door behind her. She stomped into the kitchen where she found Daisy.

"Why are you looking so angry?"

"He's a bit rude."

"Why?"

Lily repeated their conversation.

"Try something different. Just go out there and act naturally. I bet you did that coy flirty thing."

Lily pouted. "I didn't."

"I reckon you did. You flirted with him and that works on people like … well, like some people we know, but the nice men probably respond to something different."

Lily was furious again with Daisy. "So go out there and change my personality, you mean?"

"If you like him just talk to him." Daisy turned away from her.

"What's got you so cranky?" Lily asked.

"You have! And I'm not the one who broke the window."

"Shh, he'll hear you."

Daisy spun around "So? Did you tell him I did it?"

Lily grunted, turned around, and marched out of the kitchen, hoping to see Elijah look at her the way other boys looked at her. It seemed that he didn't even 'see' her at all.

"Finished yet?" Lily asked as she flounced around the corner of the house.

"All done."

When she saw him smiling at her, she said, "It's nice to see your smile."

"I'm smiling because my job is finished and it's a job done well."

Lily nodded. "My parents will be pleased that you've done a good job."

"I aim to make people happy."

"Do you?" Lily stepped forward, trying to make him think of her as a pretty girl and a potential girlfriend.

He laughed at her. "What are you playing at, young Lily?"

Lily's mouth turned down. He thought of her as nothing more than a silly young girl. She opened her mouth and couldn't think of anything to say.

"I'm sorry. Is it Daisy? You're both so much alike."

She shook her head and looked at the ground. "It's Lily."

"I'll get a bag and get rid of the glass."

"Leave it. I can get rid of it," Lily said, just wanting him to go. He wasn't attracted to her, so what was the point of him hanging around?

"It's fine; I can do it," he said, heading back to the wagon.

"I'm sure you've got better things to do," she called after him.

He turned around. "Well, we did have another job come in and they're waiting for me at the workshop."

"I can do it."

"Okay. I'll see you around D—I mean Lily."

She lifted a hand in the air in a half-hearted attempt at a wave. Why didn't Elijah find her appealing? It was odd and annoying.

NANCY CAME HOME LATER that day, after the glass had already been replaced and Lily had removed the shattered pieces.

"How is Rose?" Daisy asked as she made her mother a cup of tea.

Lily sat down at the kitchen table next to their mother. "I still can't believe you visited them without us. It was Daisy's idea, too."

"I thought it might teach you two a lesson."

Lily grimaced. "A lesson in what?"

"If you haven't figured that out yet, maybe you need some more lessons like that."

Daisy pulled a face at her sister, communicating to her to be quiet. "Go on, *Mamm*, how were Rose and Tulip?"

Lily pouted and crossed her arms over her chest.

"Rose and Mark are buying their own *haus.* They'll be

in it before their firstborn comes. You should've seen Rose's face. She's so excited."

"We would've seen her face if you had allowed us to go with you," Lily said.

Nancy stared sternly at Lily. "You should've thought of that before you broke the window."

When her mother turned back to Daisy, Lily rolled her eyes as she mouthed what her mother had just said—making sure her mother didn't see, of course. "When we are no longer under 'house arrest' we shall go and see her by ourselves," Lily told Daisy.

"Okay. I'll look forward to that."

When Daisy was seated and they all had tea, Nancy said, "Elijah came to fix the window, I see."

"Why didn't you tell us he was coming?" Daisy asked.

"Did he fix the window? It looks like it's done."

Lily answered, *"Jah, Mamm,* it's all fixed and it's as good as new."

"I didn't tell you because I wanted you to be yourselves when Elijah came here."

Lily and Daisy exchanged looks, not knowing what their mother meant and not wanting to ask.

"Who else would we be, *Mamm?"* Lily asked.

"He's nice, don't you think?" Nancy looked at Daisy first and then her gaze rested on Lily.

"Jah, he's nice," Lily answered.

"Gut! I've invited the Bontragers for dinner next week."

"All of them?" Daisy asked.

"Jah. And I've also invited Valerie and Bruno."

Daisy smiled upon hearing that Bruno would be

joining them. Her mother always had a plan for everything she did. Did she think that Valerie and Ed Bontrager might be a match, or Elijah and Lily—perhaps both? The smug way her mother was acting, Daisy knew she was up to something. It would do no good to ask; her mother would deny that she plotted and planned such things. She'd insist that it was too early for Valerie to consider another man. The more Daisy thought about it, the more she saw that Valerie and Ed might be a good match, but only some years along when Valerie adjusted to life without her late husband.

"Why are you staring into space, Daisy?" her mother asked.

"I'm thinking about Valerie and if she might ever marry again."

"*Nee*, not soon at any rate. It'd be far too early for Valerie to even look at another man. *Nee*, I'm sure that part of her heart died when her husband died. Although, I never saw Valerie and Dirk as belonging together—they were an odd match."

"Who did you see Valerie with, then?" Daisy asked.

"Maybe someone like Ed Bontrager?" Lily said, causing Daisy to burst out laughing.

It was obvious that Lily had the same thoughts about what their mother was plotting.

Their mother ignored them and picked up her teacup, taking a couple of sips of hot tea while looking straight ahead.

CHAPTER 25

*W*hen Daisy and Lily were sitting in the back row at the next Sunday meeting, Daisy noticed that Lily was doing a lot of glancing in Nathanial's direction. Nathanial was sitting on the opposite side of the room, so it made it obvious when Lily turned her head to the far right to look at him. Matthew Schumacher and Elijah Bontrager were both sitting toward the front.

Either Matthew or Elijah would be a much better match. Daisy hoped her sister would listen to reason and to what people were telling her. Her sister's life would be ruined if she got involved with Nathanial. Nathanial's brother had been involved with a girl and they'd had to get married. Daisy's heart would be broken if her sister was ever placed in the position where she had to marry a man. She wanted Lily to be sensible about her choice of a husband.

There was no divorce among the Amish—there was no turning back when they made their decisions to marry. It had to be a forever choice. They both had to choose men they could grow old with because that was exactly what they would do—either that, or live in separate houses and never marry again. Daisy was more than certain that Bruno was the right man for her, and if he ever asked her to marry him, she would jump at the chance before he changed his mind. Daisy looked over at Bruno when she should've been concentrating on the bishop's words.

AFTER THE MEETING WAS OVER, Bruno asked Daisy, "How long have we got before you have to go home?"

Daisy glanced over her shoulder at her parents. "Whenever they say they're ready to go home."

"Daisy, I wanted to do this somewhere romantic, someplace where we'd both remember it forever, but my heart can't wait. Marry me? Would you consider marrying me, Daisy?"

She stared into his dark amber eyes. "I will marry you, Bruno."

They ducked behind the buggy and Bruno pulled her close to him. "I've wanted to hold you in my arms since the first time we met."

Daisy giggled, but she couldn't speak. Her tummy was full of butterflies flapping their wings hard.

"We'll talk more about this soon. Perhaps if we get a chance to be alone on Tuesday night when we're over for dinner."

"*Nee, Mamm's* invited the Bontragers—Ed and his boys. There are so many of them that I don't think we'll have a chance for a private word. I think I'll be allowed out on Thursday, though."

He took her hand and held it. "Thursday night, we'll talk more. I'll come and collect you as soon as I finish work for the day. Can you clear that with your parents?"

Daisy nodded. "Where will we live?" She didn't want to spoil the moment, but neither did she want to move away from her family.

"That's something we'll need to discuss before we speak to the bishop, or tell your parents."

"I don't know if I can keep something from Lily."

"Will Lily keep quiet about it?"

Daisy shook her head. *"Nee,* not at all."

Bruno laughed. "Try to keep it from her if you can."

"I will."

Bruno peered around the side of the buggy. "I think your parents are looking for you." He squeezed her hand. "I'll see you on Tuesday night."

Daisy nodded and went to her parents quickly before she got into trouble for going missing.

DURING THE TUESDAY night dinner at the Yoder house, Daisy could tell by the way that Ed and Valerie looked at one another that there was some kind of history between them. Perhaps they had once dated. She made a mental note to ask her mother about it later. Could Ed have been the mystery man who Valerie had loved so long ago?

When everyone had taken their seats at the long wooden table, Hezekiah Yoder cleared his throat. "If everyone can stop talking, we might say a prayer of thanks for the food."

Everyone did as he suggested and closed their eyes.

When they had all opened their eyes, Nancy said, "Everyone can help themselves, unless someone would like me to serve them? How about you, Valerie, would you like some help?"

As soon as Valerie answered that she would help herself, the room was awash with many different conversations. Bowls of mashed potatoes, coleslaw, and meat were passed across and around the table as everyone helped themselves.

The Bontrager boys were all good talkers and they were entertaining; each seemed to have a funny story to tell. Elijah seemed to be the quietest of all, or maybe it was just because he was preoccupied the whole night by Lily, who had made sure she sat next to him.

CHAPTER 26

On Thursday afternoon, Daisy waited anxiously for Bruno. She'd managed to keep their secret—the first she'd ever kept from Lily. Lily had been distracted by talking constantly about Elijah, even more so after the Bontragers had come for dinner on Tuesday night. It seemed that their mother's plan of averting Lily's attention from Nathanial had worked, and Daisy hoped that Lily's attraction to Elijah was greater than her attraction to Nathanial.

When Daisy saw Bruno's buggy approach the house, she said goodbye to Lily and her parents and headed out to meet him.

"Hello, Daisy."

Seeing his smiling face made her heart glad. She stepped into the buggy and sat beside him. "Hello."

"I'm going to take us somewhere so we can talk about our plans. Are you hungry?"

"Always."

"I'll take us to a diner so we can have something to eat while we talk."

Later, when they had ordered burgers and were sitting across the table from one another, he began, "I've given things a lot of thought and I think it would be best if we live here. I'll have to get a permanent job somewhere ..."

"Really? You'll stay here?"

"Would you have been willing to come back to Ohio with me?"

"I would've, but it would be awful to leave my *familye*, and leave Lily. We've never been apart, not even for a day."

"Problem solved. I might have a permanent job offer where I'm working now, but it's too early to tell. The boss said he'd know in a couple of weeks if he could put me on staff. I've got a small business built up back home, but I could sell that to my friend who's looking after it now."

"I thought you said your job here had already become permanent."

"I'm talking longer term. Right now it's kind of permanent for the short term."

Daisy smiled and took a deep breath. "Everything's working out so well."

"I'd have to get a *haus* here. I've nearly got a deposit saved and if I get a good price for my business, we might have enough to buy a small *haus*. It won't be anything grand, but we can do work on a place and fix it."

"We might be able to stay with *Mamm* and *Dat;* we've got loads of space."

"We could do that, or we could stay with Valerie, but neither of those options suits me. I think we need to start off life in our own place. Does it matter to you if it's only a small *haus*?"

"Anything. Anything would be perfect as long as we'll be together."

He reached across the table and took hold of her hand. "I was hoping you'd say that."

"When would we marry?"

"I figured in December. That'd give me a chance to get things organized."

Daisy added up the months. It was only four months away, but that was enough time to sew all the clothes for the wedding and give her mother plenty of time to plan everything. "*Mamm* is going to be so excited. She really likes you."

He raised his eyebrows. "That's good."

"So does everyone else."

"And you?"

Daisy giggled. "Of course I feel that way."

He smiled at her and his warm amber eyes crinkled at the corners.

ON THEIR WAY home after they had talked about their wedding and the life they'd have together, Bruno made a suggestion. "It might be a good idea if we tell your parents tonight."

"Really? So soon?"

"Don't you want to?"

"*Jah*, I'm glad. I don't think I could've kept the secret much longer."

Daisy walked into the house with Bruno. She never

thought she'd find the perfect man for her so soon, and the best thing was that her parents approved of him already.

NANCY KNEW from the look on Daisy's face when she walked through the front door with Bruno what they had come to say.

"Hello, *Mamm, Dat ...*"

Daisy had stars in her eyes as she glanced up at Bruno as the young couple stood before them. Hezekiah and Nancy were seated.

"Sit down," Hezekiah said to the young couple whose faces glowed with youthful anticipation.

Once they were seated, Bruno said to Daisy, "Do you want me to talk?"

Daisy nodded.

"I asked Daisy to marry me and she said she would."

"Oh, I'm so pleased." Nancy jumped to her feet and spread her arms out. Daisy stood up and they hugged, and then Bruno stood as Nancy hugged him. Hezekiah shook Bruno's hand and then hugged his daughter.

"That makes your *vadder* and I happy, Daisy."

Bruno chuckled. "I'm happy I meet with your approval."

Nancy took a step back. "Are you taking her back to Ohio?"

"*Nee*, I'll try not to as long as I can find work around here."

"He's going to sell his business in Ohio. He's already got a buyer."

"That *is* good news," Hezekiah said as he sat back down again.

Nancy knew Hezekiah couldn't have been more delighted, but Nancy also knew Lily would be sad. Not only would she be the only child left at home, but she'd also never been apart from her twin sister for any length of time. She'd have to watch Lily carefully to make sure she didn't jump in to a marriage and make a silly mistake just to keep up with her older sisters.

"Does Lily know?" Nancy asked.

"*Nee*, and it has been very hard to keep something quiet from her."

"What's this?" Lily asked as she walked into the room.

"I just told *Mamm* and *Dat* that Bruno and I are getting married."

Lily stopped still with her mouth gaping open. "You are?"

"*Jah.*"

"When?"

"We figure in December or thereabouts," Bruno said.

Finally, Lily smiled. "That's *wunderbaar.*" She hurried to her sister and threw her arms around her and also gave Bruno a hug. Then she sat down on the couch opposite the happy couple, in between her parents. "Does that mean you're moving, Daisy?"

"*Nee*, Bruno can find work here and he thinks the job he has now might be a permanent one."

"Phew! That is good news. Where will you live?" Lily asked.

"We'll buy something somewhere. It'll only be small to

start with," Bruno said. "Depending on how much I get for my business back in Ohio when I sell it."

"It sounds like you've got everything worked out."

Bruno nodded and gazed at Daisy. "We have."

"Probably not everything," Daisy said. "But we know what direction we're going in."

"You've set your sails in the right direction?" Lily asked with a giggle, causing Nancy to laugh as well.

"Bruno, I have to explain why we're laughing. Hezekiah always talks about sailing and rivers when he's giving the girls advice."

Hezekiah's mouth turned down at the corners as he turned his head toward his wife. "I give *gut* advice and talking about sailing is something that the girls can relate to."

"We've never gone sailing, *Dat*," Daisy said.

"Neither have I, but there is a certain life current that you can go along with or you can fight against."

"I know what you mean, Mr. Yoder. Many things can be related to water. It's a life force, and it's important which way you set your sails in life," Bruno said.

Lily shook her head. "Men!"

Everyone laughed.

LATER THAT NIGHT, after Bruno had gone home and Hezekiah was up in his bedroom, Nancy sat down in the kitchen with the twins.

"*Mamm,* we'll have to start making clothes for the wedding, but I don't want the wedding to stop us making clothes for Rose's *boppli*."

"We can do it all," Nancy replied to Daisy. "Are you feeling left out, Lily?"

Lily screwed up her face. *"Nee.* I'm happy for Daisy. Bruno is lovely. I only wish I'd met him first," she said, nudging Daisy in a joking manner.

"It wouldn't have mattered one bit because he's in love with everything about me, not just the way I look."

The girls giggled.

"I just don't want you running into the arms of a man who's totally unsuitable when Daisy gets married and you find you're lonely."

Lily's eyes sparkled. "Hopefully I won't be lonely for long."

Nancy shook her head. "That's exactly what I'm worried about."

Lily sighed at her mother's words. "I'll make a good decision."

"I hope so. There are so many *gut* men around and I hope you can sort the suitable from the unsuitable."

"Is this about Nathanial, *Mamm?* You've never liked him, have you?" Lily asked.

Nancy frowned. "It's not about liking him. He's not got a good reputation. Just ask Tulip, and then there's what happened with Daisy too."

Daisy looked down at her hands in her lap. She knew Lily didn't believe that Nathanial had tried to attack her.

"Who do you think is suitable for me?" Lily asked her mother.

"Matthew Schumacher or Elijah Bontrager. Either of them would be my idea of a good choice."

"Well, just as well it's my choice when I choose a husband."

Nancy lowered her head while keeping her eyes fixed on Lily. "What do you mean?"

"I'm saying that it's my choice who I marry, isn't it?"

"I'm only trying to protect you from making a mistake."

"You didn't make a big fuss like this with Daisy."

"I think I did."

"*Jah,* she did," Daisy said, remembering the dreadful night when she'd jumped out of Nathanial's buggy and walked all the way home.

"*Gut nacht, mudder.*" Lily stood up. "Don't be concerned about me. I've got the perfect man in mind."

"Who?" her mother and Daisy chorused.

"You'll both have to wait and see. You didn't tell me you were getting married to Bruno, Daisy. I was the last to find out, so you'll be the last to find out when I get married." Lily flounced out of the room.

"Well, what do you think of that?" Nancy asked Daisy.

Daisy shook her head. "I didn't mean to upset her."

"It couldn't be avoided. Who was she talking about just now?"

Daisy bit her lip and thought of all the men who paid her attention. "From the way she was talking, it's not Nathanial."

"I agree."

"I hope she makes the best choice."

"I'm sure she will, *Mamm.*" Daisy stood up, leaned over, and kissed her mother on the cheek.

· · ·

Nancy sat alone at the kitchen table. She'd have Tulip talk to Lily about Nathanial—that, coupled with Daisy's knowledge of him, should be enough to change her mind about him if she still liked him.

Looking at the kitchen table, Nancy was upset that neither of the twins had thought to take their cups and saucers to the sink to wash them out. What kind of wives would they make when they had to run their own households? She'd raised them better than that. Perhaps it was all the excitement of Daisy's news that made them act in a selfish manner.

After she had washed the dishes from the tea, she walked up the stairs to her bedroom with a little smile tugging at her lips. Tomorrow she'd have Daisy's wedding to plan, and after that, she would carefully direct her remaining headstrong daughter to a suitable man—or, at least, she'd try.

Several weeks later.

Before he'd left for work, Hezekiah had brought the treadle sewing machine from one of the spare rooms to the living room. The twins and their mother were settled down for a day of sewing in the living room. Fabric was spread out from one end of the room to the other. Daisy had planned to have all her sisters as her special wedding attendants, but Rose declined as the date of the wedding

SAMANTHA PRICE

coincided with her due date. Because of that, Tulip had suggested to Daisy just to have Lily. They were in the middle of sewing Daisy's blue wedding dress and a dress for Lily along with Bruno's suit, when they heard the phone from the barn.

"I'll get it," Lily called out as she jumped to her feet.

"I wonder who that could be," Daisy said.

"I hope it's not someone with a problem," Nancy said. "I'm too busy to help them today."

"Lily and I can do the sewing if it is."

Lily rushed back inside. "It was *Onkel* John."

"What's happened?" Nancy asked.

"It's Aunt Nerida. She fell off the roof and is in the hospital."

Nancy leaped to her feet. "Is she going to be okay?"

"*Jah.* She's got a broken leg. John called from the hospital and they're fixing it now."

"Call me a taxi, Lily. I must go to the hospital and see her."

Lily ran out of the room and Nancy raced upstairs to change into clothes more suitable for being seen in public. Once she had a nice dress on, and her hair properly fixed under her *kapp,* she headed downstairs.

"Do you want us to come with you, *Mamm?*"

"*Nee,* you two keep sewing or we'll never get it all done."

"But we want to come with you," Lily said.

"It only takes one of us and she's my *schweschder,* so you two continue on here and I'll tell you how she is when I return. If I'm late, don't forget to start cooking the evening meal."

"We will, *Mamm*," Daisy said.

On the way to the hospital in the taxi, Nancy was worried. If Lily had been correct in saying that Nerida had fallen off the roof, she could've died falling from such a height. And what if she had died before they had made amends? Nancy was thankful that they had talked recently, and each had made an effort in getting back to the relationship that they once had.

Nancy made inquiries at the front desk and was told that Nerida was still in the emergency area. Without waiting for permission, she hurried to the area marked 'emergency.' Making her way through the curtained-off beds, she heard John's voice behind a curtain. She pulled the curtain aside and saw Nerida lying on the bed.

"You came," Nerida said, looking up at her.

Nancy stepped through the curtain and closed it behind her. "Of course I came." She turned to John. *"Denke* for calling and letting me know."

"It's a bad break," John said.

"It's broken in a couple of places. I landed on a cement feeding trough that John was about to move."

"What were you doing on the roof?"

"Cleaning out the gutters. The trees are so close to the house and with all the rain we had recently damp patches started appearing on the edges of the ceiling."

"Oh, that's not good."

"I told her she should've waited for me to do it," John said.

"You have too much to do already," Nerida told him. "I won't be doing it again, that is for sure and for certain," Nerida said.

"Are you in pain?" Nancy asked her.

"Only when I move. It'll probably be set in plaster. They're deciding what to do with me now."

"It'll either be that or a steel rod or two," John said.

Nancy shook her head. "I find it hard to believe you got up on the roof."

"I didn't get on the roof. I just put a ladder up to the gutters and then emptied them. I do it all the time."

"Nancy, we both have something to ask of you, if you wouldn't mind."

"Anything, anything at all."

"Would you look after the girls until I'm back on my feet?" Nerida asked.

Nancy thought it an odd thing to ask because their two girls were more than old enough to look after themselves. She had to agree because of the rift that she was trying to mend. "We'd love to have them come stay. Is that what you meant? You want them to stay with us?"

"*Jah*, if you wouldn't mind. We know you're busy with Daisy's wedding and Rose's *boppli* due soon. It's asking a lot."

"*Nee*, it's not. I would be more than happy to have them stay. Daisy and Lily would love it as well. And we've got more than enough spare rooms. They can have a room each."

John chuckled. "Don't look after them too well or they might not want to come back."

Nancy giggled. "Don't worry, there'll be more than enough chores to go around with Daisy's wedding coming up. How long will you be in the hospital?"

"It depends what they need to do to get me better. If

they put those rods in, I could be in for a lengthy stay. I'd like to know the girls are looked after, and I need John by my side. I'm not *gut* with hospitals, or pain."

"Where are Violet and Willow now?"

"They're at home," John said.

"Shall I collect them on the way? From here the taxi would go right by your place."

"I can bring them over tonight when I leave here," John said.

Nancy figured John might want to say goodbye to them and tell them exactly what was going on with their mother, so she didn't insist on collecting them.

"I should go. I don't want to get in the way when the doctor comes back."

"Okay. *Denke* for coming to see me, Nancy. It means a lot."

Nancy turned to John, "Bye, John."

"I'll see you tonight some time, Nancy. I'm not sure when."

"Okay." Nancy leaned over and gave her sister a quick kiss on her forehead before she left.

WHEN NANCY WALKED through the front door at home, the two girls looked up at her.

"You weren't very long, *Mamm*," Daisy said.

"How is she?" Lily asked.

Nancy collapsed into a chair. "She's got a bad break and they might have to put rods in her bones to hold them together."

Lily screwed up her face. "Oooh, that sounds awful,"

"Jah, it wouldn't be very pleasant at all. The good news is that Violet and Willow will be coming to stay with us until Nerida gets better."

"That's *wunderbaar.*" Lily clapped her hands while Daisy agreed.

"We'll have to make up two beds for them with fresh linen."

"I can do that," Lily said.

"Aren't they old enough to stay at home on their own? *Onkel* John would be there too. I mean, I'm pleased they're coming to stay, but it's odd," Daisy said.

"Nerida asked me and she needs peace of mind. She knows if they're with me, they'll be fine. She wants John to stay by her side at the hospital."

"I can understand that," Daisy said.

"I'll go and put fresh linen on the beds now," Lily said as she jumped to her feet.

"Can I get you something to eat, *Mamm?*" Daisy asked

"Jah. I'd like that and a hot cup of tea."

"You sit down and don't do anything until you recover. You look pale."

Nancy sat down while one daughter made the beds and the other one got her something to eat. Sometimes the twins surprised her and on a day like today, she needed all the help she could get with the shock of her sister falling off the roof.

IT WAS JUST after they finished eating dinner that night that John and the girls arrived.

"Denke for having us," Violet said to Nancy when she walked through the door with a small bag under her arm.

"Jah, Aunt Nancy. *Denke* for having us stay," Willow added.

"It's our pleasure. Any time." She looked up at John. "Have you had anything to eat yet?"

"Jah, I've already eaten."

"We had dinner ready for *Dat* when he came home from the hospital."

Willow said, "He was gone so long that we were worried about him and didn't know what had happened. Half the time we waited in the barn so we could answer the phone quickly."

John explained, "I was calling them, but someone hadn't hung up the receiver properly and that's why my calls weren't getting through."

Nancy looked over her shoulder when she heard the twins greeting their cousins. "Girls, show Willow and Violet to their rooms, would you?"

"Jah, Mamm," Daisy said.

Hezekiah walked out of the kitchen and shook John's hand. "Can you sit down with us, or are you tired from your day at the hospital?"

"I can stay a few minutes. I am tired."

"How about a hot cup of tea?"

"That would be appreciated, *denke,* Nancy."

John and Hezekiah sat in the living room while Nancy made the tea. When she heard laughter coming from upstairs she wondered what she had gotten herself in for, going back to having four girls under the one roof. The blessing of the situation was that if the cousins were still there after Daisy's wedding it meant that Lily wouldn't be the only girl left at home. The cousins would be good company for Lily.

~

The Wedding Day

DAISY OPENED her eyes to see three sets of eyes peering back at her. "What are you all doing?" They were her two cousins and her twin sister, Lily.

Lily bounced up and down on her bed. "It's your wedding day."

"*Jah,* and the sun's shining. It's gonna be a *gut* day," Willow said.

Daisy glanced out the window between the gap in the curtains. There was rarely sun at that time of year. "There's no sun."

Willow giggled. "The sun is shining in your heart because you're so in love with Bruno." She drew her hands to her heart and fluttered her lashes, causing Violet and Lily to laugh.

"How about some privacy?" Daisy asked.

"You won't have any privacy when you're married living in that tiny *haus* that you and Bruno bought," Lily said.

Daisy groaned and pulled the sheet over her head. Lily promptly pulled it away. "Get up."

"*Jah,* rise and shine," Willow said.

"We'll make you breakfast," Violet said.

"We don't want you fainting on your wedding day from lack of food," Lily said, pulling the covers off Daisy all together.

Daisy knew she couldn't win against the three of them. "Okay, okay, I'm coming. I'm getting out of bed right now."

"Don't get changed into your wedding dress yet or you might spill something on it," Lily suggested.

"Jah, I was just going to put my dressing gown on for the moment and eat breakfast in that."

"Let's go," Lily said as Violet grabbed Daisy's dressing gown and handed it to her.

"What about a shower? You don't want to be all stinky," Willow said.

"I had one last night," Daisy replied.

Willow frowned.

"Do I smell, or something?" Daisy sniffed the air.

"Nee, but have another one anyway."

Daisy sighed. "I'll eat, then shower, and then one of you will surely tell me what I should do after that."

The three girls giggled while Daisy pulled on her dressing gown.

"Aren't you excited, Daisy?" Willow asked, as the three of them followed Daisy down the stairs.

"I am. I never thought the day would come. I've been looking forward to it for months."

"You'll be a married lady in a few hours," Violet said.

"Jah, you'll be Mrs. ... What's his last name?" Willow asked.

"Weber," Lily said.

"You'll be Mrs. Weber. Mrs. Daisy Weber. Or, Mrs. Bruno Weber. How does that make you feel, Daisy?"

"Um, old, I guess."

Nancy walked into the kitchen as the girls were eating. "Hurry up, girls. In just under an hour the benches and tables are arriving. How are you feeling, Daisy?"

Daisy knew her mother was stressed with so much work needing to be done to get the house ready for the hundreds of guests who'd be attending the wedding that morning. "I'm getting a little nervous now."

"You should be. Marriage is a big step."

"Denke, Mamm," Daisy said.

"Not to be taken lightly," her mother added.

"Jah, Daisy knows all that, *Mamm.* You're only making her more nervous," Lily said.

"Lily, have you seen your *vadder* this morning?"

"Nee, I only just woke up. Is he missing?"

She shook her head. "I think he's outside somewhere."

"Have you and *Dat* eaten, *Mamm?"* Daisy asked.

"Jah, we ate earlier." Nancy hurried out of the kitchen.

"Your *Mamm* seems more nervous than you," Willow said to Daisy.

"She was like this at Rose's and Tulip's weddings too. She likes everything to be just so and she won't let anyone else do anything."

Lily added, *"Jah,* and she has to be in charge of everything. The big boss lady."

Daisy finished the last mouthful of food. "I'll talk to *Mamm."* She hurried out of the kitchen while she heard Lily grumbling about having to do the washing up.

Daisy found her mother heading up the stairs. *"Mamm."*

Her mother looked behind her. *"Jah?"*

"Can we talk?"

"Okay." She turned around and came down the stairs. "I thought you'd want to talk sooner or later."

They sat on the couch together. "This will be the last time I talk with you as a single woman."

Nancy nodded and took a deep breath. "Well, I've had this talk with Rose and then with Tulip."

"What talk?"

Nancy frowned. "About what to expect on your wedding night."

Daisy was horrified. *"Mamm!* Stop it."

"Stop what?"

"I know about all that stuff." Daisy put her hand to her head.

Her mother looked relieved. "You do?"

"Jah, I've heard all about it and I know what to expect, so stop worrying." Daisy put her hand over her mouth and giggled.

"Well, you might laugh, but no one bothered to have that talk with me and it was a shock to me on …"

"Enough!" Daisy blocked her ears. "I don't want to hear it, *Mamm."*

Nancy laughed.

When Daisy took her hands away from her ears, she said, "I didn't want to talk about that. I just wanted to say *denke* for being such a *gut mudder.* I hope that I will be just as good with my *kinner."*

Nancy stared at her and Daisy could see her mother's eyes become misty.

"*Denke*, Daisy. I did my best. I did my best with all of you. Sometimes I was sure you girls must think I'm just a cranky old cow."

Daisy giggled. "Well, sometimes. I'm only joking. You were never a cow, and never too cranky. Just normal cranky when we did horrible things." Daisy hugged her mother and Nancy hugged her back.

Hezekiah walked in the front door. "The men are here with the benches. Daisy, you're not dressed!"

"It doesn't take me long to get ready."

"You better go now," Nancy said to Daisy.

The other three girls, all giggling and seemingly talking at once, came out from the kitchen into the living room.

"Take Daisy up and help her get ready, girls," Nancy ordered.

The four girls ran up the stairs while Hezekiah and Nancy smiled at one another. A wedding day was a good day.

DAISY RAN her hands over the soft fabric of her blue wedding dress. One cousin braided her hair while the other tied her pinafore apron at her back.

Lily stepped back and looked at her sister. "You look beautiful."

"You would say that, Lily, because you look exactly the same," Violet said.

Lily giggled. "I know that, silly."

"Anyway, you do look beautiful, Daisy."

"Denke, Violet." Daisy put her hand on her stomach to quell the nerves that had just kicked in. She hoped she'd feel better when she saw Bruno. He was her dream come true.

Nancy poked her head through the door. "Five minutes."

"I'm nearly finished with her hair," Violet said.

"Oh, Daisy, that looks lovely. The dress turned out really well."

Daisy breathed out heavily and was just about to say something to her mother when she shut the door.

"Mamm's more nervous than you are, Daisy."

"Only five more minutes," Daisy muttered to herself.

"Five more minutes to change your mind," Willow said.

"Willow, that's a dreadful thing to say. Why would she change her mind? She wants to marry Bruno, don't you Daisy?" Violet asked.

The cousins' squabbling made Daisy laugh. "I do want to marry Bruno. And I won't be changing my mind."

Violet shook her head at her younger sister.

Once Violet finished braiding Daisy's hair, Lily placed the white organza prayer *kapp* on top of Daisy's head.

"There you go, even more beautiful," Lily said. "Now let's go."

Daisy went down the stairs first and Bruno was waiting at the bottom. The room was buzzing with low conversations and crowded with many people. As Daisy's gaze swept over the benches, she saw that every space was

SAMANTHA PRICE

filled. There were even people on the porch and lining the sides of the room.

They walked to the front and stopped in front of the bishop. After a quick glance behind her, Daisy was comforted when she saw her mother and father. They'd sat next to Bruno's parents. Tulip and Rose were there with their husbands, and her two older brothers were there with their wives. Rose was looking particularly glum and very, very pregnant.

It seemed as though Rose was still a little cross that Daisy hadn't waited to have the wedding until after her baby was born. Daisy figured she'd waited long enough to marry Bruno and she couldn't wait a few more weeks to start her new life.

Malcolm Tyler, who had a rich baritone voice, was chosen to sing a hymn in High German. Daisy closed her eyes as she listened to his beautiful lilting tones. When he was finished, the bishop delivered a short sermon on life and marriage. Then he read verses from Genesis and told the story of how man was created in God's image. Then the time came for Daisy and Bruno to exchange their agreements with one another. They were finally pronounced married.

Daisy looked into Bruno's amber eyes and thought back to the first day she saw him. In her heart, she'd known even back then that there was something special about him. Another thing that made her pleased was that her mother hadn't pushed them together, and neither had her mother met him first. Daisy had found him all on her own, and somehow, that had made everything that little bit more special.

. . .

LATER WHEN THE wedding feast was underway, Nancy was distressed to see Nathanial continually looking in Lily's direction. "There is no way on *Gott's* green earth that I will ever allow Lily to marry that man."

Hezekiah replied, "What are you talking about, Nancy? Matthew would be perfect for Lily. If another woman doesn't …"

Matthew Schumacher was Mark's younger *bruder* and Mark had married their oldest daughter, Rose.

Nancy frowned and looked over at Lily again to see Matthew sitting next to her. Seeing Matthew and Lily talking happily distracted her from her dislike of Nathanial. "I've always liked Matthew."

"I've always liked him too," Hezekiah said.

Nathanial now had competition in winning Lily's heart. And both Matthew and Nathanial had to watch out for Elijah Bontrager.

"Just as well Violet and Willow have come to stay. Lily will need the distraction of more girls in the *haus.*"

Hezekiah shook his head. "More girls in the *haus?* Is that what we really need?"

"That's what we've got until Nerida gets stronger and her leg mends. And I think it's a blessing for Lily to have the girls there."

Laughing, Hezekiah reached out and took hold of Nancy's hand. "One day we'll be on our own again, but it might be in our old, old age. If we last that long."

"I think you might be right, but I'm grateful for every day we've got together."

"Me too. You've made every day of my life much brighter since I met you. You've made me a happy man."

Nancy was too choked up to speak. If she lost Hezekiah, she didn't know what she'd do. All she could do was smile at him. He knew how she felt since she told him all the time. "We've been blessed," she managed to say, and he looked into her eyes and smiled.

Moments later, Nancy looked over at her newly married daughter, Daisy, who was staring at her new husband. She closed her eyes and prayed that Bruno would stay in their local community and not take Daisy back to Ohio with him. They had bought a house, but most of his family was in Ohio and that was enough for Nancy to find reason to worry. She closed her eyes again, this time more tightly, and gave her concerns to God. He would watch over them all.

"All will be well," Hezekiah said quietly.

Nancy opened her eyes and looked at him.

"Daisy and Bruno will be okay."

"I know. Daisy has made a good choice in Bruno," Nancy said.

"He's her perfect match, just like you're mine."

Nancy giggled like a young girl. Hezekiah always made her feel better. She took her mind off scenarios that might never occur, and concentrated on enjoying the remainder of the wedding celebration. However, the cogs in the deep recesses of her mind were still turning over regarding Lily —her next matchmaking project. Daisy had found her own husband, but Lily sorely needed her help. That was a project for another day.

A NOTE FROM SAMANTHA

I hope you enjoyed Daisy's story. When I was a child, I wanted to be a twin. I figured I'd always have a best friend. Twins have always fascinated me, and that's why I have featured them in some of my book series. The twins, Lily and Daisy, have a plan for their future, but it doesn't work out. They aren't going to marry brothers or twins and live in the same house or even close by. Now Lily must make new plans for her future.

Samantha P

www.SamanthaPriceAuthor.com

AMISH LOVE BLOOMS

Book 1 Amish Rose

Book 2 Amish Tulip

Book 3 Amish Daisy

Book 4 Amish Lily

Book 5 Amish Violet

Book 6 Amish Willow

Box Set Volume 1
Contains books 1 - 3

Box Set Volume 2
Contains books 4 - 6

Made in the USA
Columbia, SC
22 November 2023

26949269R00131